DARK WINGS

RITE WORLD: FALLEN ANGEL
BOOK 1

JULIANA HAYGERT

COPYRIGHT

RITE WORLD

Welcome to the RITE WORLD!

For a printable reading order, click here!

Free Novellas:
The Vampire Hunt
The Light Witch

Novellas:
The Hunter Path
The Light Calling
The Light Witch
The Wicked Alliance
The Shadow Fae
The Fae Queen

The Wild Wolf
The Vampire Princess
Snow Hunt

Rite World:
The Vampire Heir (Book 1)
The Witch Queen (Book 2)
The Immortal Vow (Book 3)
The Warlock Lord (Book 4)
The Wolf Consort (Book 5)
The Crystal Rose (Book 6)
The Wolf Forsaken (Book 7)
The Fae Bound (Book 8)
The Blood Pact (Book 9)

Rite World: Blackthorn Hunters Academy
The Demons Kiss (Book 1)
The Hunter Secret (Book 2)
The Soul Bond (Book 3)
The Shadow Trials (Book 4)
The Immortal Vow (Book 5)

Rite World: Vampire Wars
The Darkest Vampire (Book 1)
The Darkest Witch (Book 2)
The Darkest Magic (Book 3)

Rite World: Night Wolves
The Night Calling (Book 1)
The Night Burning (Book 2)
The Night Hunting (Book 3)
The Night Rising (Book 4)

Rite World: Lightgrove Witches
The Midnight Test (Book 1)
The Midnight Spell (Book 2)
The Midnight Flame (Book 3)
The Midnight Secret (Book 4)
The Midnight Hunt (Book 5)
The Midnight Wish (Book 6)

Rite World: Fallen Angel
Dark Wings (Book 1)
Light Magic (Book 2)
Fallen Demon (Book 3)
Wicked Angel (Book 4)

And more to come!

AUTHOR'S NOTE

DEAR READER,

THIS BOOK IS THE FIRST IN A SERIES ABOUT ARIELLA, A FALLEN angel who was featured several times in the Rite World universe. She first appeared in *The Wolf Forsaken*, which is part of the first Rite World series, and she has had small and large cameos in almost every series since.

You might be wondering if you need to read the previous books to enjoy this one. The answer is no, you don't. I planned this book to be a good entry point into the Rite World.

However, my hope is that you fall in love with this world and its characters and want to read the other books and series. If that's the case, you'll find the link to the Rite World reading order at the back of this book, along with lots of extras.

Enjoy!

—Juliana

1

I LANDED A NICE UPPERCUT TO THE GUY'S CHIN, MAKING HIM stumble two steps back. Taking advantage of the way the inside of his head rattled right now, I advanced on him, locked a powerful hook to his cheek, and finished with a side kick to his stomach.

He went down with a groan.

The crowd roared and shook the wire cage fence.

The referee started counting. "Ten, nine, eight ..." he went on, but the guy didn't get up. The referee grabbed my arm and raised it high. "And the winner is Arwen!"

I almost winced at the fake name. I had been using it for the last three months, and I still hadn't gotten used to it. The crowd's screams echoed through the underground fight club, hurting a little.

Not liking the attention, I pulled my arm down and marched out of the cage. The public advanced on me, but when I glanced at them with a frown, bared teeth, and my bloody fist raised, they let me pass.

I weaved through the cheering humans, disappearing

through a thick metal door and into a large room with a big glass wall. Mr. Green sat in a leather chair, holding a glass of whiskey. Two of his goons stood behind him while he watched the crowd through the one-way glass.

He smiled at me.

Mr. Green was a short man with a generous belly and receding hair line. He wore fancy suits and acted as if he wiped his ass with money. I was sure Green wasn't his last name, but a moniker he had adopted when he entered this life. This was only one of the handful of illegal cage fighting clubs he owned in Houston, and I had heard he had a few more in Dallas.

I didn't smile back.

"Dear Arwen." Mr. Green raised his glass at me. "Another win. Well done."

"Thanks." I extended my hand to him. "I want my money."

His smile got a millimeter smaller. "Why the rush? You're doing well. You should do another fight tonight."

I shook my head. "That wasn't the deal. I told you I would do one fight a week, that was it."

And it was already too much. My body hurt all over and I needed rest ASAP.

Mr. Green tsked. "My offer still stands. Become my official fighter, come fight for me every night. You'll make a lot of money." His smile was gone now. "You need money, don't you?"

I jerked my hand out some more. "That's why you'll pay me for the fight right now."

"So impatient." He pulled an envelope from inside his jacket and lifted it up. One of his goons grabbed it, walked over to me, and slapped it into my open hand. I glanced inside the envelope to make sure it was all accounted for. "I'm a man of my word, Arwen. It's all in there."

A man of my word, my foot.

When I first came to the fight club, he had wanted to hire me to waltz around the cage between fights, wearing a bikini that barely covered anything and shaking my ass as if I was looking for some.

I glanced at the glass and could see three young women doing exactly that. Word was he pushed himself on all of them.

I wanted to break his neck.

He left me alone, though, once I proved I could fight.

"I'll see you in a week," I muttered, unhappy about that prospect.

I walked to the only other door in the room, which led to a short hallway. Two doors were always locked, but the other led to the lockers and restrooms.

I slipped inside the locker room, grabbed my duffel bag, changed my dirty tank top for a thin sweater, my leggings for black jeans, my sneakers for my boots, put on my hooded black leather jacket, untied my long, silver-blond hair, and stuffed the money in the bag. After a quick stop by the restroom, where I cleaned my face and made sure I didn't have any blood on my clothes, I continued down the hallway to the last door: the back alley.

As I was exiting, three men walked in—I had fought against two of them, and I knew I was going to fight against the third one next week. I had won all of the fights so far and didn't expect to lose anytime soon.

That, though, didn't buy me any friends. Not that I wanted any.

The three men glared at me. One of them, Jonas, even stood in my path for three seconds.

My first instinct was to blind him with light.

But I couldn't do that anymore.

I sidestepped him before I did something stupid, and with my head down, exited the alley onto a dimly lit street in one of the shadier neighborhoods of Houston.

I didn't like being in a big city, but I didn't have much choice. I needed money, and in a small town, it would have been hard to be a nobody.

I knew this wouldn't last, though. Maybe another six months? A year? Not more than that. Then I would have to move again to stay out of sight, and continue pretending I was a regular human.

With a groan, I hiked my duffel bag onto my shoulder and walked to the bus stop. I rode the bus to a better side of town, where there was a great noodle place I had found by chance, and it was now my favorite restaurant.

Not that I had tried many.

I took my usual spot in the corner and my usual server, Laurah, a lady who was probably over sixty years and wore a style of makeup from the eighties, came to ask if I was going to have the usual.

"You know it," I said, finally relaxing.

She winked at me and went back to put in my order.

I reached into the duffel bag and checked to see if the envelope with my money was still there. Of course it was, but I couldn't help it.

I had been on Earth for five years. I had to learn how to take care of myself, and after so many years at the Guardian Academy, I had become rather good in physical combat, even though it was rare for my kind to fight like that.

I shook my head and closed the duffel bag. It was stupid for me to go down this road again. What was done was done. All I could do was lay low, keep my head down, and survive.

Pretending I was a freaking human.

Laurah brought over my noodles and my sweet tea, and after trying to make small talk and not getting anywhere with me, she left me alone. I ate slowly, enjoying this meal before I went back to Crosby, a small town about thirty minutes east of Houston, where I lived.

Or rather, where I hid.

Houston was good for fights and meals, but it was terrible to stay off other supernaturals' radars. In Crosby, no one knew me. I came to Houston, made my money, ate, talked to the witch who made my potions, and went back home where I hid for another week.

What a great life.

I finished, placed a twenty-dollar bill on the table, and picked up my duffel bag. Halfway through standing, I felt a chill slither down my spine.

I sat back down, my eyes wide.

I didn't have my magic anymore, but I knew what it meant.

Two Seraphim walked past the restaurant. One of them glanced through the large glass windows, but I pulled my hoodie over my eyes, pretending I was still eating.

When I looked up, they were gone.

I glanced around, alarmed. Of course, no one else noticed. Humans couldn't tell angels or other supernaturals from humans, but for some reason, I could.

Besides, one of the Seraphim was Julien, a male who had been a year ahead of me at the academy. Thankfully, he hadn't been the one who had spied inside the noodle shop or I was sure he would have recognized me, hoodie and all.

Holding my bag, I shot to my feet and scurried to the restroom in the back of the shop. Right beside the restroom was another door labeled "Employees Only." I knew it led to the kitchen and a back door, which opened to a parking lot shared with the sports clothing store on the other side of the block.

I opened the door and stepped into the kitchen.

The cook looked up and glared at me. "You can't be back here!"

Laurah saw me. "Dear, let me—"

"No!" I snapped. "I just saw my ex." I made sure to look afraid and made my voice tremble. "He ... he wasn't a nice man. I need to go, but I don't want to run into him."

Her eyes filled with pity. Done.

"Of course, dear." She put a hand on my shoulder. "Go through the back. Just this once, okay?"

"Thank you!"

I heard the cook's protests as I rushed out of the kitchen and raced across the parking lot to the store on the other side. I entered through the side door and slipped in unnoticed.

The shoe store had a couple of clients and more staff than necessary. I pretended to browse the sneakers, but a sales associate kept close to me, probably wary of me hiding under my hoodie with my bag slung across my body.

I shuffled closer to the front of the store and looked out the large glass windows.

Just then, another two Seraphim walked by.

"She has to be around here," Izrail said. He had been two years ahead of me in the academy.

"Her aura doesn't feel right," the other one said. I had

seen him before graduating, but I didn't know his name. "She must have been here days ago and left a trace."

Shit.

I grabbed a pair of shoes and sat with my back to the window. As I pretended to try on the bright orange sneakers, I reached inside my bag and closed my hand over the small glass vial. I pulled it out and looked at it. I had only a sip or two left.

Frowning, I took half a sip.

That should do the trick.

Julien came running after Izrail and the other. "Hey, I can't feel her aura anymore."

"See? I told you it's probably days old," the other said. "We're wasting time here."

"We're following whatever clues we have," Izrail said. I glanced over my shoulder and saw him close his eyes and inhale deeply. I stilled, praying the damn potion was strong enough. Five seconds later, he opened his eyes. "You're right. It's too faint. She must have been around here but she's long gone."

"I'll tell the others," Julien said before running off.

Soon, Izrail and the third angel walked away.

I let out a deep breath.

"May I help you?" a girl asked. She was wearing the vest with the store's logo on it. The other sales associate was still close by, her eyes on me.

My will was to rush out of the store, but chances were there were still some angels in the area, even if they were all about to leave.

I pointed to the orange sneakers in my hands. "Do you have this one in blue?"

She gestured to the shelves behind her. "What you see is what we have."

"Ah, shame." I put them down. "I'll try these anyway."

I quickly realized I had gotten a size too big and the girl, who continued looking at me, must have noticed. Thankfully, she didn't say anything.

I stood, walked a few steps to the side, looked in the mirror at the end of an aisle, and made my way back to the bench, while glancing out the window.

The angels were nowhere to be seen.

I took the shoes off, put my own boots back on, and stood again. "Thanks," I muttered as I walked past the girl.

She muttered curses under her breath, thinking I couldn't hear her. I might have lost my magic, but I still had an incredibly good sixth sense, increased agility, sight, and hearing.

Bitch, she had called me.

Well, to be honest, she wasn't wrong. Probably everyone I had met in the past five years thought I was a bitch. And the angels sure thought a lot worse of me.

I exited the store, checked the vial again—this half dose wouldn't last me a week.

Time to get some more.

2

I had heard from Sylvie who heard it from a half-siren who had heard from another witch. When I first showed up at her door in Cloverleaf, a small town between Houston and Crosby, she had tried shooing me away, pretending she was appalled that I had called her a witch.

When she threatened to call the police on me, I caved.

"I'm an angel," I told her. "Well, a fallen angel." That hurt to admit. "And I need your help."

Every supernatural knew a fallen angel was a disgraced angel who had lost her wings and couldn't go back to Elysium —the place humans called Heaven. Putting on my best sad face, I told her I had lost my Celestial Sword when I lost my wings, and my magic had been stolen from me.

She had taken pity on me and let me in.

And now I depended on her.

I drove my car to her house, parked in the driveway, and weaved through the forest of her front yard—way too many plants for such a small place.

I almost tripped on a thick branch jutting from the forest into the small stone path, and then bumped into a wall.

"What the—?"

I looked up and I stilled.

The wall was a man.

A handsome man in a black suit and with deep blue eyes stared holes into me.

I took a step back and opened my mouth to apologize, but he beat me to it.

"Watch your step, sweetheart," he said, his voice deep and charming. Then, he flashed a brilliant and perfect white smile at me.

I didn't like it.

I frowned. "You're the boulder in the way."

"Is that so?" The corner of his lips tugged up as he took a large step aside, almost stepping into the vegetation surrounding us. "There you go, sweetheart."

My frown deepened. Shaking my head, I walked past him, and made it to the front door. Despite myself, I glanced back at the man.

But he was gone.

What the hell?

I knocked on the door.

Ten seconds later, Sylvie opened it wide. "Did I miss—?" Her face fell when her eyes met mine. "Oh, it's you."

"Were you expecting someone?"

"I thought—" She shook her head. "Never mind. What is it that you want now?" She turned her back to me and disappeared through the doorway to the right.

I closed the door behind me and followed her from the foyer into her work area. The place was as full of stuff as her yard was full of plants. Long wooden tables with all kinds of herbs and ingredients, ranging from bone powder to bats' wings and mouse tails. Old, moldy books lined the shelves on the far left, and in the back of the room, three cauldrons stood side-by-side—a small, a medium, and a large one.

The medium cauldron was bubbling with dark green liquid.

"You know what I want," I said.

The old witch rounded one of the long tables, reached for a thick stack of a weird-looking plant, and started chopping it into tiny pieces with a cleaver.

Sylvie was probably almost two hundred years old, with long silver hair tied in a braid, and many wrinkles. She wore dresses from the last century, topped by thin scarfs, usually dark red or indigo.

Today she wore a dusky pink one.

I had asked before what kind of witch she was, and what coven she belong to.

"Have you heard of lone wolves?" she had asked me. "I'm a lone witch."

And that was all she ever said about the subject.

It was clear she didn't like me, or anyone for that matter. But like me, she needed money to survive, and the only thing she knew how to do were potions and elixirs.

"I need more." I fished my latest winnings from my duffel bag and slapped the bills on the table in front of her. "How many doses can you get me with that?"

She glanced at the money, then at me. She pursed her lips and continued chopping the plant. "Three."

"Three?" I almost shrieked. "The last time you made six!"

"Well, the main ingredient is Mage Bloom, a rare plant, and my supplier increased its price." She stopped chopping and stared at me. "I need to pass that price to my customers."

Damn it.

Three doses wouldn't last a week. To have more money, I would need to agree to more fights. Mr. Green would love that.

I sighed. "Fine. Give me three. I'll come back in a few days with more money for more."

"I can give you one now. Come back for more—"

"What? Why just one?"

"Didn't you hear what I said? Mage Bloom is rare. Why did you think the price went up? It's hard to find. I have only enough for one. My supplier will bring more by Wednesday."

Her supplier was a little goblin who dealt with dark magic. My gut had tightened when I learned who he was, and I had almost given up on this deal. But I needed this potion.

I swallowed my pride and made a deal with her: I paid her well and she made me a potion to hide my aura from other angels.

Now, it seemed, I would have to pay her better than well.

I shook my head. "I can get the money for more, but if this plant is so rare, money won't matter."

"I'm afraid not."

I took a couple of steps back and sat on the armchair beside another table—a thick leather ledger was open on top of the table, and there was a lengthy list in a language I didn't understand.

What could I do? Without this potion, I had no way of hiding from the angels. And today, I had proof that I really needed it. I had been taking half doses to make it last, and the angels were on my tail.

If I stopped taking it, I was done for.

"There has to be something I can do," I muttered to myself. I glanced at Sylvie as she put the pieces of chopped herb into a small bowl. "You don't know any other suppliers? Or witches who could have other contacts, someone who can find more of the rare plant."

"I actually contacted a witch I know," she said. I stared at her with wide eyes. "What? I knew you needed it." She turned her back to me and spilled the chopped plants into the bubbling cauldron. Smoke rose high and a sweet, flowery scent filled the room. "Anyway, she didn't have any and said she hadn't been able to secure any in months."

"If we can't find the plant, then we need to create another potion, with other ingredients."

She chuckled, not amused. "You think potion creation is easy, Ariella?"

I almost winced at the sound of my name. I probably shouldn't have told her my real name when I first met her, but sometimes, even I made mistakes.

Hell, scratch that.

I made mistakes all the damn freaking time.

"I know it isn't," I said, dejected. But what else could I do? I needed a solution. "You don't know any genies, do you?" I joked.

Genies were tricksters and I wouldn't deal with one even if my life depended on it ... And we were getting to that point.

"Well, I don't know a genie, but I know a higher demon who grants wishes."

I stilled. "What?"

"Didn't you see a man walking out of here just before you arrived?" She placed a big wooden spoon on the cauldron and mixed the liquid.

"Yes."

"He's a powerful demon who deals with wishes."

I almost turned around and ran out, but he was long

gone. Besides, he was a demon. He was probably worse than a genie.

"What's the catch?" I asked, not able to let this go so easily.

"He always asks for something in return."

"Like what?"

"It varies from person to person. Or from supernatural to supernatural. It's rare for humans to know about him. Anyway, I heard he sometimes asks for a specific job to be accomplished, some help with something, special items, or ... even for the supernatural's soul."

Of course. Why would a demon do anything out of the goodness of his heart?

"That's too big of a price."

She brought the spoon up and sniffed the liquid. "Still, if you change your mind, you can find him at one of the VIP booths at the Nine Club in Houston. He's always there."

I shook my head once. That was absurd. I wouldn't deal with a demon, much less sell my soul to him.

"Just ... get my potion ready, please." I pointed to the money then to the cauldron. "I need to go make more of that, so you can make more of that for me."

She tsked. "I have never met such a rude angel before."

Oh, boy, she had no idea.

THE ENTIRE WEEKEND, I WENT BACK AND FORTH ON MY decision.

Could I continue fighting? Could I fight more times a week to make more money? And what if I made all the money I needed and Sylvie didn't have any more Mage Bloom to make my potion? There were certain things that couldn't be conjured with magic.

Unless it was a wish.

Despite trying hard not to, I couldn't stop thinking about the demon Sylvie had told me about, the one I had bumped into outside her house, the annoyingly charming one, who obviously thought highly of himself.

If I could grant wishes, maybe I would think highly of myself too.

I hid inside my apartment for most of the weekend. I only left to run and train, to keep my body primed. I would need it, if I were to fight more often.

Damn, I missed my magic.

It would have been much easier if I could smite my opponents.

I wouldn't have been able to do that even if I still had my magic. Humans didn't know about the supernatural world and it was best if it stayed that way.

Angels were the ones who had first come up with that rule, and we had to set the example.

Even if I was an outcast and hunted by my own race now.

Finally, on Sunday evening, I caved.

I put on tight black leather pants and a tunic, my high-heel boots, and went back to Houston, to the Nine Club. I parked my car in the parking garage beside the night club and threw my charm at the bouncer to let me cut the line.

Thankfully, I was considered pretty for a human: long, silver-blond hair, silver-gray eyes, and a toned body. I had applied a little makeup and even painted my lips burgundy.

This demon and his wishes better be worth this trouble.

The bouncer smiled at me and let me pass. I heard the protests coming from the others, but I didn't care. It used to bother me. Angels were supposed to care. Angels were supposed to be good, kind, nearly perfect.

I had lost almost all of that in the five years I had been stuck on Earth.

The club was like many others: a dance floor in the middle, tables to one side, a long bar on the other, and a VIP area on the second floor, giving the patrons a perfect view of the crowd from above. The loud music thrummed through my body, and the scent of alcohol and perfume was heavy in the air.

I stopped at the edge of the dance floor and looked up.

Instantly, I saw him.

Leviathan, the wish granting demon, stood in the center

VIP booth with a whiskey glass in his hands. Two women wearing red dresses danced beside him, and two males were with them.

I let out a long breath and headed upstairs.

On the way, a few men stopped and looked at me. Some even attempted a lame line. I ignored them. I would rather face a handful of demons than one single drunk man. They were the worst.

I was stopped by another bouncer at the entrance of the VIP booths.

"Do you have an invitation?" he asked.

Damn it. "No, but—"

"You can't enter without an invitation." He straightened and looked straight ahead, over my head.

I narrowed my eyes. If I had my magic ...

I shook my head. I couldn't think like that. I didn't have my magic. I was useless like a human, and I needed to think like one. I put a hand on my waist, shifted my weight, pushed my hips to the side, and did a small hair toss. Wearing my award-winning fake smile, I batted my eyes at him.

"Are you sure I can't come in?"

He glanced at me, his eyes running the length of me. He opened his mouth, closed it again. "I—I can't."

Shit.

I stepped closer to him. "But you see—"

"Arwen!" someone said from behind me. Startled, I turned and saw Mr. Green standing there, two of his goons flanking him. "What a surprise to see you here." He walked up to me and patted the bouncer's chest. "It's okay, Pete, she's with me."

The bouncer moved aside and Mr. Green gestured for me to follow him.

This was not how I planned to do this, but if it got my foot in the door, then so be it.

I followed Mr. Green to his VIP booth, which was right beside the demon's. I looked at the demon, but he was busy talking to the other males. Were they all demons? Or was he scamming humans?

A server showed up as soon as Mr. Green and I entered his booth. She handed him a martini and asked me what I wanted.

I almost said nothing, but I didn't want to stand out. "Red wine, please." She nodded and left.

Mr. Green sat in the booth, closer to the railing overlooking the dance floor and stared at me. Not liking this one bit, I took a seat across from him, my back to the demon's booth.

"I've never seen you here before," Mr. Green said. "Is this your first time?"

"I've come here a couple of times," I lied. "I'm not big into going out." That wasn't a lie. "I prefer training."

"Right. So you can win your fights." He leaned forward, one of his elbows resting on his knee. "My offer stands, Arwen. Tell me what it'll take for you to fight more than once a week."

Here was my chance.

I glanced over my shoulder. The demon had sat down and was talking to another male. The two girls in red dresses hovered close by.

I frowned and faced Mr. Green. "Once a week is enough —for now."

Hopefully, I wouldn't have to do it at all.

"You're a mystery, Arwen." He tilted his head and a small smile spread over his lips. "I like mysteries."

I suppressed a shudder, lest my current employer see how much he disgusted me.

Two men entered Mr. Green's VIP booth: Carlos and Jonas, the jerks from the fighting club.

"Look, it's Princess Arwen," Carlos said. He grabbed my glass of red wine from the server and sat beside Mr. Green. "Didn't expect that."

Jonas sat beside me. "Me neither. I thought the little princess would be training nonstop." He turned a deadly eye at me. "I still want a rematch."

Mr. Green chuckled. "Come on now, boys. We didn't come all this way to talk about work."

"Of course not," Carlos agreed, but his expression read murder.

I bet I could kick both their asses at the same time, and something in me wanted to challenge them right here, right now, but I didn't want to waste time.

I was here for something else.

"Excuse me," was all I said as I got up and walked away from the booth. I turned to the demon's booth.

The women were now dancing around the other males, but the demon wasn't there. I glanced around and saw his black-haired head going down the stairs.

I started after him, but the demon was slippery.

The humans seemed to part for him to pass, while they crowded around me, slowing me down. If I had my magic, I would smite them all and—

I stopped that thought. No, I wouldn't smite them all. That was not what an angel did. I had spent way too much time on Earth and with other supernaturals. Their ways were clearly leaving a mark on me, and not a good one.

The demon was tall, taller than most humans, and I saw his head across the dance floor, heading to the exit.

Shit.

When I finally made it outside, I glanced around and didn't see him anywhere. There was still a short line before the bouncer, hoping to get in, a couple crossing the street to the parking garage, and nothing else.

I had lost the freaking demon.

I fished my phone from where I had tucked it into the waist of my pants and searched for Sylvie's number. She was sure to know where else I could find him. If not today, then tomorrow, or sometime this week.

I would have more of her potion on Wednesday, but I couldn't go on like this. I couldn't fight to get money and spend almost all of it to buy a potion to mute my aura, so I could keep on hiding from the angels for the rest of my life.

That wasn't living.

Besides, it was harder and harder to find Mage Bloom?

I needed a better solution.

Then it hit me that it was almost midnight. Should I call the witch at this time? Would it be rude? Did I care about being rude? Usually, I didn't, but what if I upset her and she delayed my order?

Defeated, I started walking back to the parking garage beside the club. A narrow driveway divided the club building and the garage, and as I walked across the driveway, a light shone over me.

Panic took over and I put my hands up, ready for a fight.

It was the angels. They had found me.

But nothing happened.

When I lowered my hands and my eyesight adjusted, I

saw it was the headlights of a black car a few feet into the driveway.

And a figure leaned on the car's closed door.

Leviathan.

I stood there, perplexed.

"Sweetheart, I might consider this stalking," he said, his voice as deep as I remembered.

I pointed to the three-story garage. "I was walking to my car."

"Aren't you the one who bumped into me outside Sylvie's house?"

I hesitated. "Yes."

"Didn't you sit down beside *my* VIP booth and make small talk with a human?"

Damn it. "Yes."

"And when you saw I was gone, you followed me." He pushed away from the car, reaching his full height. "Confess it, sweetheart, you're after me." He took two steps toward me. "Why?"

I walked to the side, closer to him, mostly to get out of the range of the headlights, and halted only four feet from him.

Despite myself, I took him in. It was impossible not to.

Hell, the demon was more than handsome.

His face alone was one of a god, not a demon. He had black hair, longer in the front, almost to his eyes, shorter in the back, and it framed a sharp face with five o'clock shadow over his chiseled jaw and chin. His nose was straight, his eyebrows thick, and his full lips a pale pink.

Tonight, he wore an indigo suit with a silver shirt, three buttons open, revealing a little of the strong curve of his chest muscles. Though I had no idea what he looked like under those clothes, I would bet he was ripped. His suit, definitely designer, fit well around his wide shoulders and thick biceps.

But what attracted me the most were his eyes. A bright, baby blue so pure and luminous, it was hard not to stare.

What the hell was I thinking?

I shook my head, trying to get rid of such ridiculous thoughts. Who cared what the demon looked like? He could be as ugly and nasty as Mr. Green for all I cared, as long as I got what I wanted out of him.

"I heard you grant wishes," I said.

"That's not exactly what I do, sweetheart, but sure, it's something like that."

"I want you to grant me a wish. What's your price?"

"I like to know who I'm dealing with before I make a deal."

I hesitated. Should I give him my fake name? No, if he was going to grant me wishes, he probably needed my real name. "I'm Ariella. And you're Leviathan."

"Nice to meet you."

Enough with this shit. "So, about my wish."

His eyes narrowed. "Tell me what you need, sweetheart."

"I'll tell you only if you grant it."

"I'll only know if I can grant it if you tell me what it is."

Damn. I wasn't planning on rendering the details of my problem to him. I shifted my weight. "I'm an angel and I lost my wings. I would—"

"So, a fallen angel."

I gritted my teeth. "Yes. Five years ago, a higher demon took my wings, and a handful of months ago, another demon stole my powers—"

He scoffed. "So, you're practically human."

I clenched my hands into fists. "Does it matter to you what I am?"

"I need to know who and what I'm dealing with."

"I'm a fallen angel without her powers. Happy?" I wasn't.

"What rank are you? Or should I say, *were* you?"

Oh, so he knew about that? I didn't think many demons knew about our ranks.

From the bottom, we had angels. They didn't have powers and their wings were a lot smaller than the others. They were good people who only wanted harmony and peace. It was said the first humans were actually angels who wanted to explore Earth. In the years they stayed here, they lost their wings and became humans.

If an angel had light magic and demonstrated stronger feelings that were not lined up with pure goodness, they were sent to the Guardian Academy, to become Guardians and fight evil. In the academy, we were taught to use our feelings in the right way.

Before demon hunters existed, we were the only ones fighting demons and evil beings on Earth. I had heard that because there was so much evil on Earth and the angel population was small, Adona had decided we couldn't fight alone. She sent an archangel to a human and gave him powers—the first demon hunter.

If that was true or not, I didn't know.

When an angel graduated from the academy, he was a Cherub, a new recruit. It was a proud moment when the angel received his Celestial Sword and started going on missions. After several years proving himself, gaining experience and power, he would then become a Seraph.

Another several years and experience later, and a lot more power, he would become an archangel, the strongest and most powerful of all angels. The generals and commanders in our armies.

And at the top, was our own god, Adona, the most pure and kindhearted and righteous creature to ever exist. She was as old as the universe.

I shifted my weight, uncomfortable with this conversation. "I'm a Cherubin." I had graduated from the academy when I came down to Earth for a mission and became stuck here.

"Then you're young, sweetheart." Yes, I was. Twenty-three years old, but I felt ninety after so long on Earth. Angels aged like humans until we became archangels, when they became practically immortal, like Adona—but only one percent of us ever got to that rank. "Where's your sword?"

He knew too much about us. A lot of our lives and systems were a mystery to others. But this demon knew a few things.

"The same demon who ripped my wings off destroyed my sword."

"And you won't ask me for it?"

My eyes widened. "Can you get it back for me if I wish for it?"

"Is that what you want, sweetheart?"

"I want my wings and my magic back," I said. Of course, I also wanted my sword back, but I had seen Molraz destroy it. I always thought I couldn't get that one back until Leviathan mentioned it. "Bonus points if you can find the higher demon who took my wings and give me a new Celestial Sword."

Slowly, the demon walked around me and I felt like a dead piece of meat at the butcher.

"What's the name of the demon?"

"Molraz." It could have been me, but I felt as if the demon had faltered when rounding my back. "Do you know him?"

"I know of him, yes," he said, his words clipped. "I can find the wings and the demon, but I can't restore your magic and I can't give you your sword back."

My brows slammed down. To fight against the angels, to find out what mess I had been unwillingly thrown into, I would need my magic back. As for my sword, it was a shame, but maybe when I returned, when I straightened everything out, I could get one back.

My wings and the higher demon were a good start.

"And the price?"

He stopped in front of me, closer this time, and the corner of his lips tugged up. "You have two options, sweetheart."

By the light, this sweetheart thing was getting on my nerves.

"And they are?"

"One, you work for me for ten years."

"So I'm practically yours?"

His blue eyes became even brighter. "Exactly. After that, you're free to do whatever you want."

Belonging to a demon for that long? Yeah, right. Pass. "And option number two?"

"You can do whatever you want for ten years, I don't care, but after those ten years, your soul is mine."

"My soul? You mean, my soul when I'm dead?"

He nodded.

All right, so, I either belonged to him for ten years, or I would be dead in ten years.

None of these were good options. "And a third option?"

"No third option, sweetheart. You're already getting one too many."

"Yeah, that won't work for me." I turned my back to him and marched away.

When I glanced over my shoulder, I saw him entering into his car—a sleek black Porsche.

I shouldn't have hoped this would work. Dealing with demons was always a bad idea, why did I think this time would be any different? I wasn't this naive.

I would have to fight, get the money I needed, and find a second supplier or witch to make my potions. After that, I didn't know. I still didn't like the idea of hiding my entire life, but I couldn't perform miracles on my own.

Especially not without my magic and my wings.

As I approached my car in the garage, I called Mr. Green. He was probably still inside the club.

He picked up on the second ring. "Arwen, what is it?" he yelled over the loud music in the background.

"Call your club. I'm on my way there for a fight."

4

Since coming to Earth five years ago during my failed mission, losing my wings and my sword, and getting stuck here, things hadn't gone my way.

But lately, it was getting worse.

I had gone to the fight club that night, secured a fight for three in the morning, won, and got more money. The next day, Mr. Green called me to say he was glad I would be fighting more.

I wasn't.

Then on Wednesday, I visited Sylvie to get my potion. After she handed it to me and I paid, she looked at me with huge eyes full of pity.

"I'm afraid my supplier couldn't find more Mage Bloom," she said. It was like a punch to the gut. "He said he'll keep trying, but it might be another two weeks, maybe three." She paused. "Or more. He really can't be sure."

This wouldn't work. The potion I had bought would last five days comfortably, maybe eight days if I took smaller doses. But when I did that, the Seraphim came to Houston, right at my tail.

How long would it take them to find me this way?

No, I had to do something else.

An idea sparked in my mind, but it was crazy. I went back to my apartment and slept on it. Next morning, I woke up, went for a run, showered, had my breakfast, and that crazy idea was still the only one I had.

Without a choice, I packed my duffel bag with a couple of changes of clothes, toiletries and whatnot, and hopped in my car. If this worked, I wouldn't need Mr. Green anymore. If it didn't, I would be back before Friday night and ready for another fight.

It took me five and a half hours to drive to New Orleans. I arrived in the city in the middle of the afternoon and went directly to the Midnight Cauldron in the French Quarter.

The place was still the same: a square room that I bet would look big without all the knickknacks crowding, but with the many tables and shelves displaying all the fake products—and some not so fake—the place felt tight and almost suffocating. As I walked to the back, I noticed a basketful of voodoo dolls to my right, and wishing bones in a jar to my left ... was that real frog legs? I shuddered. Yeah, definitely this kind of magic wasn't for me.

The owner stood behind a counter in the back, ringing up a couple who had a bagful of her goods.

I waited at a good distance until she was done with them. As soon as they walked away, she turned to me. "Good afternoon, child. How have you been?"

A wide smile stretched over her face, the pearl white of her teeth in contrast with the darkness of her skin. Khalisa played the part of the witchdoctor well, with locks on her long black hair, and dresses that reminded me of old barmaids in pirate movies. She wore a lot of jewelry around her wrists, neck, and ears, which clanked with each of her movements.

Once upon a time, Khalisa had been a Wildthorn witch. For some reason, she had left her coven and learned voodoo magic. She still had contact with her old coven, and several other covens in North America.

The last time I had seen Khalisa had been several months back, when I was searching for Molraz and following the trail of a demon group who had dealt with him before. I had brought another angel here, Zadkiel, who I had believed had been dead long ago. He had escaped from the underworld and was looking for a demon.

As usual, Khalisa knew it all. If she didn't, then she found someone who did.

And that was why I was here.

"Not so well," I confessed. There was no reason to lie to the witchdoctor. She always remained as neutral as she could in the supernatural world, and she helped anyone who came to her.

Her smile faltered. "What happened, child?"

A lot. In the last year alone, I had been captured and tortured by warlocks who wanted to steal my power. When I was rescued, I helped my newfound friends fight them. Then I had helped a wolf shifter pack search for a damn dragon and defeat a former prince of the underworld—and lost my magic in the process.

And now I couldn't help anyone anymore.

"Too much," was all I said. I didn't want to go down memory lane and bring back so many bad feelings and thoughts. "But I had an idea to reverse my situation and I was hoping you could help me."

She narrowed her eyes. "Tell me."

"I've met this wish demon, Leviathan. I need him to grant me a wish, but his prices are too high. I know there are powerful summoning and trapping spells ... I was wondering if you knew one so I could summon the demon and trap him in a witch's circle, or something."

A knot formed between Khalisa's brows. "And then?"

"Then I'll make my wish, and he'll need to grant it, because the price will be his freedom. Can you do that?"

"No." She shook her head vehemently, and my shoulders deflated. "That's dark magic. I don't deal in that. We would need a dark witch for that or a light witch who can perform dark magic."

I perked up a little. "Are you saying this is doable? That you know someone who can do this?"

"We'll see." She picked up her cell phone from under the counter and pressed a couple of buttons. "Hello, child," she said to the phone after someone picked up. "I was wondering if we could meet this evening. Either here or at the Light Castle." She paused as the person on the other side spoke. "No, nothing urgent, but my guest might not want to wait too long." Another pause. "All right, my child. We'll be here." She put down the phone.

"What just happened?" I asked.

Khalisa smiled at me. "The dark witch is coming."

The dark witch wasn't coming for a while. I went for a walk around the French Quarter and bought some beignets. It was impossible to come here and not eat some.

I hadn't been to New Orleans a lot, but each time I came, I had been shocked by how many supernaturals roamed around the French Quarter as if they were humans—and I couldn't even sense them all.

Supposedly, the supernatural community in the entire world was negligible compared to humans, but in places like this, I wondered if that was really true.

When I went back to the Midnight Cauldron, I helped Khalisa sort some inventory. Boxes of fake voodoo dolls, bead bracelets, and skeleton keychains had arrived and they needed to be entered in the ledger. I told the witchdoctor about using a computer and software and internet for this, and she dismissed me.

"I'm old, child, older than you think," she said. "I'll die doing things the old way."

Thankfully, it worked. As I busied myself, the time passed.

And then at closing time, a young woman and a man entered the shop.

"There you are," Khalisa said to them. "It's good to see you."

"You too," the young woman said.

Khalisa locked the front door and flipped the open sign to closed, then gestured to me. "This is Ariella, a fallen angel." I winced at the introduction. "Ariella, this is Hazel, Queen of the Lightgrove Coven, and Sean, the Head of the Light Order."

My eyes widened. Oh, I had heard of them. Apparently,

Hazel had become queen in December, and some of my friends had attended the coronation.

Hazel was pretty with blond hair and pink streaks, a few piercings, and blue eyes. She wore a gown that somehow mixed the old and new styles and looked amazing on her. Beside her, Sean was handsome with chestnut brown hair and blue eyes. He looked regal in a white leather uniform and a sword at his waist.

"Nice to meet you, Queen Hazel. Sean." I didn't know if I should bow or what.

Hazel offered me a smile. "Hazel is fine. Now, tell me, you needed my help. With what?"

I told her what I had told Khalisa, but I went further this time. "Five years ago, I came to Earth for a mission with my colleagues. A higher demon called Molraz ambushed us. He killed everyone, and he would have killed me, but I was able to escape, though not before he destroyed my sword and ripped my wings off." I could still feel that horrible pain and agony. I thought I would die right then. "I want to find the demon and my wings."

Sean frowned. "To get revenge?"

"I want my wings back. Without them, I can't go back to Elysium."

"Can't you contact them at least?" Hazel asked.

I shook my head. "I've lost my magic."

Hazel's eyes widened. "What?"

"When I was helping the Nightshade pack defeat Paimon, he stole my magic."

"You're going to ask Leviathan to grant your magic back?" Sean asked.

I shook my head. "He said he can't grant that, but he can find my wings. And that's better than nothing."

"Right." Hazel nodded. "Once you have your wings, you can go back to Elysium. There, you can explain what happened and they will know how to restore your magic?"

I didn't think restoring magic was in their know-how.

I couldn't simply go back there. Not if I wanted to keep my head and neck attached to my shoulders.

I had a lot to do first.

"Right," I lied. "Can you help me?"

Hazel looked at Sean. Something passed between them, a nonverbal communication and understanding, and they both nodded at the same time.

"It's a difficult spell, but I can try," Hazel said. I let out a long, relieved breath. She glanced at Khalisa. "Can we use the basement?"

"Of course, child." She walked past a curtain of beads over a doorway and led us to the back room, where I had worked on the inventory.

One of the doors to the side opened to narrow stairs leading down. Khalisa turned on the lights and was the first down. We followed her into the basement: a large open area, with lots of stuff along the walls—old books and furniture, folded boxes, boxes full of what looked like clothes, and more.

Khalisa went to a broken desk in the corner, opened the drawer, and grabbed black chalk. She handed it to Hazel.

"Thank you," Hazel said.

She knelt on the floor and drew a large, black witch circle. It had three interconnected rings, and several runes and symbols between the rings. Lastly, she drew a large five-pointed star that reached the outer ring, and Khalisa placed lit black candles where the star and the circle converged.

She handed a small pouch to Hazel, and she spread a silvery powder around the circle.

Meanwhile, I had to refrain from pacing or biting my nails.

This was a lot of preparation to summon a damn demon.

Hazel turned to me. "Now, the last part." She gestured for my hand. I laid my hand on top of hers. "I need a few drops of your blood." She produced a small dagger out of nowhere. "May I?"

I nodded.

She pricked my finger with the blade's tip. I clenched my jaw, waiting for the pain, but it was fast and faint. She turned my hand down and let the drops fall in the circle.

"Say his name," she told me.

"Leviathan," I said, firm. Strong.

Then, Hazel closed her eyes, lifted her arms in front of her, and chanted in Latin.

A sudden rush of air whipped around us and the candles flickered. The silvery powder on the floor glittered, and the black circle lines shone dark.

The wind blew stronger and Hazel's voice grew louder.

"He's fighting me," she said through gritted teeth.

Sean put a hand on her shoulder. "Borrow my energy."

"No." She shrugged him away. "I need hers." She closed her hand around my wrist and squeezed hard.

I opened my mouth to tell her she just needed to ask, but her grip tightened more and I felt it, my energy transferring from me to her and into the circle.

The wind whipped around us, almost toppling us over.

Thunder echoed through the ceiling and I looked up, eyes wide.

"It's her power," Sean told me.

The flash of lightning cut across the air above our heads and then a dozen bolts struck the circle, shaking the floor. Dark smoke rose from the ground, covering most of the circle and the basement.

With a deep gasp, Hazel let go of my wrist and fell to her knees.

"Hazel!" Sean knelt beside her.

"I'm fine," she rasped.

Good, then the next important question: "Did it work?"

"I think so ... but something felt wrong."

A shudder rolled through my body.

The smoke dissipated, revealing a figure in the center.

At least seven feet tall and wide as a bear, the figure stood in the circle, his skin pale and his muscles pulsating with his hard, enraged breathing. His arms turned black from the elbow down and his hands were long, sharp claws. He wore black slacks, which were ripped from his thick thighs to his ankle and didn't really go with the rest of the picture.

Large bat-like wings spread behind his back, as much as they could inside the circle. Sharp hooks like claws curled at the top of the wings.

Leathery horns curled around his head. His black hair was longer, down to the middle of his back, and his eyes had turned completely black—and stared straight at me.

The demon was here.

5

With a roar, Leviathan ran toward us.

Only to slam into the circle's invisible walls.

Baring his sharp teeth, he brought his hands up. Dark magic enveloped his arms and rushed to the circle.

Hazel gritted her teeth and placed a hand on the circle. Bright light shone from it, and Leviathan stumbled back, dazed with her magic.

"What happened?" I asked, confused.

The demon was here; it had worked. Nothing had gone wrong.

She glanced at me. "Can't you feel it?"

"Feel what?"

"He's stronger than I thought he was," she started. "The moment he realized what was happening, he fought me. To bring him here, I had to tether him to here, to something here, more specifically, to someone."

"What are you saying?"

"I'm sorry, but I ended up binding him to you."

"WHAT?"

At that, Leviathan stilled. He had been paying attention to what we were saying. Slowly, his demon form faded. In less than five seconds he went from being an ugly beast, to an annoyingly handsome man, who was wearing only pants.

And nothing else.

His body was pure, well-chiseled muscles.

I silently reprimanded myself for noticing.

"I'm sorry," Hazel said, looking from me to him, and back to me. "I didn't mean to. I thought it would be a line from there to here. But with him fighting me, I ended up using too much magic and I might have recited a word or two wrong."

Leviathan crossed his big arms in front of his naked, ripped chest. "I can feel it," he said through gritted teeth. "The bond."

Hell, I didn't want to be bound to him. "Can you undo this?"

"I think so." Hazel looked at Khalisa. "I'm sure the both of us can do something to reverse this."

Khalisa answered her, but I wasn't listening anymore. My eyes met Leviathan's and I felt it then, the bond. It was faint, a tiny tug in my chest. Shit, this was real.

"I'll kill you, sweetheart," he said, half-charming as he had been before, half-dead serious.

I was sure he would.

"I don't think you can hurt her," Hazel said.

I snapped my head at her. "What do you mean?"

"The bond would stop him. I felt it when it was happening. If he kills you, he'll die too."

My eyes became two saucers. "Does that apply to hurting too? He can't hurt me without hurting himself?" She nodded. "And vice versa?"

"I'm not sure. I bounded him to you to get him here, not the other way around."

Oh, that gave me an advantage, didn't it?

I approached the circle, standing half an inch from its outer ring. "You want out of there?" He didn't say anything so I went on. "Here's the deal: You'll grant my wishes, help me get my wings back and find Molraz."

His eyes fumed. "The first time, you asked me to *find* your wings, not to help you get them."

"Things changed," I said, feeling rather smug. "Grant my wishes, help me with them, and then I'll have my friends break the bond. The faster you help me, the faster you'll get rid of me." I paused for effect. "Deal?"

He paused for longer. His jaw tensed. His eyes darkened. "Deal."

"You can let him go," I told Hazel. She hesitated. "You said it yourself; he can't hurt me."

Nodding, she closed her eyes and brought her hands up. She chanted something in her witchy language. The glow of the witch's circle shone again for a few seconds, and then it was gone. The lines had all disappeared too.

Leviathan fixed his eyes on me.

His dark claws and black eyes were back as he let out a roar and lunged at me.

I stepped back, my stomach clenching.

But he never got to me.

Leviathan stood frozen, his open claws half a foot from my throat, his eyes fuming, his teeth snapping. He struggled against the bond's invisible magic.

I relaxed a little bit. It worked. He really couldn't hurt me.

Sean raised his sword. "Stop!"

"He can't hurt her," Hazel reminded him.

"He might not be able to, but he can be a prick and scare her," Sean said.

I stood tall. Me, scared? Oh, I wouldn't let them see that. "There's nothing you can do."

He pushed against it one more time. With a deep growl, he stepped back and lowered his arms. The claws and the black eyes disappeared.

"I'll get you for this, sweetheart," he said with a snarl.

"As long as it's after we find my wings and Molraz, I don't care." I kind of cared. My next step would be to restore my magic somehow, but that was further down the list.

"Do you think this bond can stop me?" He glared at me and Hazel before turning his back on us and walking up the stairs.

I watched in horror and started after him. No, he couldn't leave. He would help me, he had to help me.

Hazel put an arm out, stopping me. "Wait."

I frowned at her but did as she told me.

Khalisa, Sean, Hazel, and I waited in tense silence for several minutes. Finally, after what seemed an eternity, Leviathan stomped down the stairs again, his hand rubbing at the center of his chest.

He set his deadly gaze on Hazel. "What the hell did you do to me, witch?"

"It's the bond, and it was unintentional," she said. "When I tethered you to Ariella, I had to pull hard and short, so you would come. You can't go far from her."

"He can't?" I asked, perplexed. "What happens?"

"It fucking hurts." He continued rubbing at his chest, the same spot where I had felt the faint tug of the bond.

Ha, so I had the advantage even there? This sucky night was turning out to not be so bad after all.

"Ready for my wishes, then?" I couldn't help it; I was feeling smug. He groaned in agreement. "I wish you to find my wings and the demon Molraz, and help me get my wings back."

"And my payment?"

"I'll release you from your bond." I glanced at Hazel and Khalisa. "Right?"

"Right." Hazel nodded. "We'll work on it."

"Thanks." I turned back to the demon. "So?"

"Have you thought this through, sweetheart?" the demon asked. "What if your wings have been destroyed? What if you have been searching for something that doesn't exist anymore?"

I frowned. "I would know. I know you won't understand, but I would know. It would be like a human losing a leg. The leg is gone; there's nothing you can do about it. But with my wings ... I know they are out there. Their magic is intact." I lifted my chin and repeated, "So?"

Leviathan's eyes turned all black and he inhaled deeply. I thought he was ignoring me. I snapped my hands in front of his eyes, but nothing happened.

"I think he isn't here, child," Khalisa said.

"What do you mean?" I asked, confused.

"I think his body is here, but his mind isn't. He has gone somewhere else to grant your wish."

"What?"

"He stepped into a portal?" Hazel asked. "But inside his mind?"

"Something like that," Khalisa said.

I didn't get it, and honestly, I didn't care, as long as it worked.

Finally, after a few minutes that had felt like an eternity,

Leviathan blinked and his eyes turned their normal blue again.

"I saw your wings," he said, sounding less murderous. "They're on display in a mansion in San Francisco."

"Are they intact?" I asked eagerly. He nodded. "California?" I had been around that area before, searching for clues. But I guess without someone who could *see* my wings, I would never find them. He nodded. "And the demon?"

"I saw him but couldn't pinpoint where. But don't worry, we'll find him."

"How?"

"Just trust my magic, sweetheart." He placed a hand over his chest again. "Are we done here?"

"Yes—"

He walked away before I could finish my sentence. I stared as he went up the stairs and pointed to him. "Won't he feel the pain again?"

Hazel walked up to me. "He must have gone farther. I think upstairs is okay. He might feel the pull tighten, but not hurt."

If he hadn't been a demon, if he was a nicer character, I would have felt empathy for him, for having this unwanted bond. But I didn't. With his wish-granting powers, he must have taken advantage of a lot of people. This was some kind of punishment, and he deserved it.

"Thank you," I told them. "For the first time in the last five years, I'm hopeful."

Hazel offered me a small smile. "I'm glad to help. I'm just upset I messed up the spell."

"It's better this way," Sean said. "Then he can't hurt her."

I nodded.

Khalisa approached us. "Find your wings, child, and don't worry. While you're gone, we'll find a way to break the bond."

"We'll also research how you can recover your magic," Hazel said.

My heartstrings tugged. "That would mean a lot. Thank you."

After a quick goodbye, I walked out of the shop. Since it was past midnight, the French Quarter was quieter, but not completely asleep. A few bars and suspicious shops were open, and a dozen people walked down the street.

I glanced around, searching for Leviathan.

"Right here, sweetheart," he said from behind me. He leaned on the shop's wall, his arms crossed. Like a snake, he slithered to me.

I held my ground, not wanting to show him that despite knowing he couldn't hurt me, he scared me. "Ready to go?"

He flashed that sinful half grin of his. "As much as I know you're enjoying the view, I need some clothes, sweetheart. Then, we can go."

6

"Sweetheart, can this old junker go any faster?"

Leviathan was a real player. His tone and the fake smile on his face, the way he turned his torso toward me in the passenger seat, it was all perfectly measured. But his words had a bite to them, revealing how much of a jerk he was.

We had been on the road for fifteen minutes in my old Civic, headed toward Houston, and I was already regretting this entire deal. If this demon continued this game, I would strangle him in no time.

He couldn't hurt me, but I was sure I could hurt him.

"Just ... sit back and relax," I told him as I stepped on the gas. I wouldn't go a lot over the speed limit for a freaking demon.

Since we had summoned him when he was alone at home, Leviathan didn't have anything with him other than the ripped black slacks, so we ended up going back to Khalisa's for the night. She didn't have a room at her shop, but there were couches in the back room, and we rested there until morning. She also found a t-shirt and sweatpants for the demon, for which he didn't even thank her. In the morning, we entered the first shop we saw, and Leviathan bought himself some slacks and a button-up shirt. At first, he had asked me to pay for them.

"Hell, no," I told him once I saw the price tag. I didn't have that kind of money.

Leviathan charmed the female sales associates and convinced them to let him just give them his credit card info for the payment.

Once we were outside, I asked why he didn't wish for clothes or money.

"I can't use my magic on myself, sweetheart. If I could, I wouldn't be in this situation." He winked at me, but I could see that under that flirting, he was still furious with me.

Well, we had over five hours until Houston, which he insisted we stop at. If it depended on me, we would go directly to San Francisco, but Leviathan was adamant about it. Plus, if we chose the southern route, Houston was practically on the way, sooo …

"Sit back and relax? It's Thursday morning, sweetheart. I have business waiting for me." He reached into the center console and grabbed my phone from its stand. "Speaking of which, I need to make some calls."

"Hey! I need that!" My old Civic didn't have a screen and I couldn't hook up my phone on it for the GPS. I had to look directly at the phone, thus the stand.

"We will be on this interstate for over two hundred miles, sweetheart. Just drive."

I opened my mouth to object, but he raised his hand between us and spoke into the phone.

I gripped the wheel hard so I wouldn't reach across the seats and land a punch on his chin.

Bastard.

He made the first call and started working. I turned on the radio in the car and raised the volume so I couldn't hear him. If he was dealing in more wishes and taking advantage of others, I didn't want to know.

Leviathan threw me an irritated glance because of the music, but he turned his back to me and stared out the window, while talking about meetings and clients. I focused my attention on the road and the songs, though here and there I heard Leviathan talking other languages. Was that French? And Russian? And Mandarin?

Angels knew all languages, but when my magic was stolen, that ability went away with it.

It was despairing, to be an angel and *not* be an angel. Things had been bad before, when I had lost my wings and had the other angels hunting for me, but it got exponentially worse when I lost my magic too.

No, I wouldn't focus on the dreadful things.

Finally, I had something going for me. Leviathan knew where my wings were, and I would soon have them back. That was the first step of many. Hazel and Khalisa said they would research a way for me to get my powers back—I didn't even want to think about that. It made me giddy, and I was afraid of getting too excited, only to be disappointed if they couldn't do anything for me.

First, wings.

Second, Molraz.

The rest, I would figure out later.

We only stopped once to get gas and a bathroom break. We arrived in Crosby at almost two in the afternoon. Since we would be away for a few days, I needed to pack a bigger bag. I also needed a shower.

Thankfully, Leviathan waited in the car. I really didn't want him to see my shoddy apartment. I had rented it not even four months ago, and had bought only a mattress, an armchair, a small TV, and a stool for the bar area in the kitchen. That was it.

After all, I never planned on staying, on settling into a human life. Even if I never got my wings and my magic back, I would have to move every few months. In fact, now that I had seen the Seraphim, it was probably time to get going.

When I went back to the car, Leviathan entered an address on the map app on my phone, and we headed to downtown Houston. The address led to a high-rise building, and Leviathan told me to enter the underground garage.

He directed me to the visitors' parking spaces, then told me to follow him. A doorway led to a small sitting room with a sofa that looked modern, but probably uncomfortable, and two golden-trimmed elevators. Leviathan glanced at a camera in the top corner of the room and nodded.

On the elevator, he positioned himself in front of the panel and entered a series of numbers—like a password. Then he pressed the button for the twentieth floor, the last one.

The elevator opened to a short hallway and gray double doors. Leviathan pressed his thumb to a keypad, entered another password, and the doors clicked opened.

I followed him inside but couldn't stop gawking.

I had expected a super luxurious penthouse with fifteen bedrooms, nineteen bathrooms, rugs and curtains.

The place was one giant rectangle, about twenty feet tall, and mostly surrounded by glass.

To the left, there was a rug and a huge gray sectional in front of a pillar, from which hung a ninety-inch TV. To the right was another rug, a bed that had to be custom made, because it was double the size of a normal king, two night-stands, and an armchair. Farther to the right, there were four doors and I was assuming one had to be the bathroom. Leviathan disappeared inside one of those doors and I got a peek—it was a closet.

In the center was the kitchen comprised of gray counters. The tallest thing in there was the fridge, which was against another pillar. But everything was top notch: the appliances were stainless steel and looked too expensive to touch. Even the stools around the counter that formed a seating area were big and heavy, giving the impression that each of them cost thousands of dollars.

The place smelled like him: a deep wood, spicy, and musk scent, masculine and good on him.

While he was gone, I spun around, amazed by the simplicity, and yet elegance of the few things he had in this place. The floors were light gray marble, the walls between the giant windows and the pillars were that industrial concrete look, but it worked.

There were no frilly decorations, no superfluous stuff, and lots and lots of open space and natural light.

I walked past the kitchen and went to the windows. You could see the entire city from here and it was beautiful. Breathtaking. After a moment, I turned around and looked at the apartment again.

This place was awesome.

Leviathan walked out of the closet, and without his shirt, entered the bathroom. I could hear the water running, so I went back to the window and focused on the view outside. It was hard, though, knowing his glorious body was naked behind a thin door.

I shook my head. What the hell was I thinking?

He might be hot, but I had seen plenty of hot men before and had not lost my thoughts to desire so easily. Besides, he was a demon who takes advantage of others. Ninety-nine percent of demons deserved to be dead or in the underworld, imprisoned for eternity.

After fifteen minutes, Leviathan exited the bathroom with damp hair and wearing crisp, dark blue slacks and a white shirt. He reached inside the closet, grabbed a small, wheeled suitcase, and left it beside the front door.

He turned to me. "I know the view is great, sweetheart, but it's time to go."

I cringed. "Can you stop calling me that?"

With his half-grin, Leviathan asked, "Why, sweetheart?"

Groaning, I walked toward the front door, but didn't give him an answer. If he had half a neuron, he knew why.

"Not that way." Leviathan sidestepped me and walked back to the four doors. He grabbed the knob at the third door. "Through here."

"What do you mean?"

"Come on, sweetheart." He opened the door and stepped into the darkness.

Where the hell was he going? I followed him, but halted when I walked through the doorway and total darkness surrounded me. A feeling like I had been in a twister hit me hard and fast.

Then it was gone.

I blinked and found myself past a door and in a large, musky room. There were no windows, though the ceiling was high, and a few naked bulbs hung from wires.

In the center of the room, a man was tied to a metal beam.

"Has he said anything?" Leviathan asked, and only then I

noticed there were three men in the room, a safe distance from the other one.

"No, sir," one of them answered.

My gut hardened. What was I seeing?

Leviathan tsked. "Igor, Igor. I've tried being nice, my friend, but you're forcing my hand."

Nice? I took a few steps to the side, to take a better look at the man tied to the beam—his face was lolled to his chest, and blood stained his white shirt.

Leviathan had tortured him. Or his goons had.

And he had brought me here.

"What the hell are you doing?" I asked, approaching the scene.

"Stay back, sweetheart." Leviathan pointed at me but kept looking at the tortured man. "This demon has a taste for angels."

The man's head snapped to me and his eyes—completely black—fixed on mine. His long, forked tongue slithered out and licked his dark lips. "Angel," he hissed, dragging the vowels.

A shiver rolled down my spine.

Leviathan glared at me. "Stay. Back."

I wasn't afraid of a demon, especially one that was tied up and beaten, so I held my ground. Mostly to defy Leviathan than anything else.

"Sweet angel," the demon said.

Leviathan walked up to him and punched him squared on the cheek, forcing the demon to turn his head. "You look at me, trash. You answer to me. Where is it?"

The demon licked his lips again. "Give me that angel, and I'll tell you everything."

Leviathan's hands enveloped in darkfire—a demon's dark magic. "I won't ask again."

A low chuckle came from the demon.

Leviathan drew back to punch him again, but the demon pulled up his legs and kicked Leviathan in the chest, sending him back a few steps.

Taking advantage of those precious seconds, the demon pulled hard on the chains tying him to the beam. The beam, which seemed like a sturdy piece of metal, groaned and bent under the effort, and the chains loosened.

The demon crawled up the broken beam, twisted his arms under himself, and got free.

He lunged at me.

I raised my fists and held my ground. I may not have my magic, but I wouldn't run from a fight.

I punched the demon when he was close, but he didn't budge.

"What the—"

He was stronger than he had let on. When Leviathan hit him, he had not resisted. Now, he felt like a boulder under my aching hand.

Before I could finish my sentence, the demon closed his hands around my neck and drove me to the floor, slamming my back and head against the concrete.

My vision darkened and pain exploded through me.

I fought for consciousness and kicked the demon, but he was strong.

His mouth opened wide, his many sharp teeth around that nasty tongue.

I screamed, throwing all of my strength against him.

The demon flew back.

Dizzy, I sat up.

Had I done that?

Then I saw it. Leviathan had wrapped the demon in darkfire.

"Like I said, I tried being nice," he said before forming a stake out of darkfire and driving it into the demon's chest.

The demon let out a piercing shriek and I covered my ears. Then, he crumpled to the ground in a messy heap.

Leviathan staggered to the side. Blinked twice.

His goons ran toward him. "Boss?" one asked, reaching for him.

Leviathan raised his hand. "I'm fine." He blinked again; his eyes found mine. "It's your pain and dizziness I'm feeling. Are you fine?"

My mouth opened. Then closed.

Oh, wow, for a moment there, I had forgotten he could feel whatever I felt.

I nodded and pushed to my feet. Everything went dark, but I recovered. "I'm fine," I said, seeing as Leviathan was almost to me.

He stopped abruptly.

As if nothing had happened, he turned to his goons. "Clean up and find me another. I'll be back in a few days. A week at most."

"Yes, sir," the goons answered in unison.

Without ceremony, Leviathan walked back to the door we came through and opened it for me. "Ladies first."

7

ON THE WAY TO HOUSTON, LEVIATHAN HAD WANTED TO BUY airplane tickets, first class, to go to San Francisco, as it would be faster, but I reminded him I wasn't really a human, and had never bothered making any documents, not even fake ones. If I got in trouble, my magic could solve anything. Now, I stayed under the radar.

It was better this way—harder for the angels to find me.

He thought about making fake documents for me, but that might take even longer, or rent a charter plane, but he couldn't book one as fast either, so we decided to drive all the way to San Francisco.

"But we'll go in my car," he said.

So now we were inside his sleek, red Ferrari—the black one I had seen before had been parked beside this one—driving out of the garage under his building. We had come back to his apartment through the door-slash-portal and immediately exited it with Leviathan's suitcase, grabbed the elevator, and hopped in the car.

All the while, Leviathan didn't say anything and I lagged a few steps behind.

I had killed people before, mostly supernaturals with evil intent. But this time, it had been different. I knew no background other than that demon liked to eat angels.

Another shudder coursed through me as I remembered being shoved to the ground and not being able to get free.

"Are you cold, sweetheart?" Leviathan asked, his tone light, flirty.

I frowned. "You said you felt my pain, my dizziness when the demon got to me. What else do you feel?"

His whole body stiffened and his grip on the wheel tightened slightly. "I feel your presence. If I'm too far away, even when I was taking a shower, I felt the pull toward you. I'm sure that if we found a maze and you ran from me, I could easily find you." He paused. "I feel your pain, probably a little less than you do, and when I focus, I can get hints of your emotions."

"What?" I sat up straighter. "I don't need you spying on me like that!"

"Not my fault, sweetheart. You're the one who put this fucking spell on me." We stopped at a red light and he glanced at me. "I know you hate this bond almost as much as me, and I could feel the fear growing inside you ever since I killed that demon."

I adjusted myself on the seat, uncomfortable with this topic. "Why did you kill him?"

He snorted. "Because he was about to kill you."

"No, you know what I mean. Why did you have him in that room, tied up and tortured? What information were you trying to get from him?"

The light turned green and the car started moving. For a moment, I thought he would ignore me.

"My business is complicated and has nothing to do with you," he said, serious. I probably could count on one hand the times he had been serious with me so far. "It's better if you don't know."

I didn't like the sound of that. It only made me more wary of him.

And he probably could feel that.

Damn it.

Surprising me, Leviathan veered onto a smaller road and into a gas station. Without another word to me, not even a glance, he parked beside a pump and got out to fill up the car.

I knew he would drive for hours nonstop if he could, so I decided to use the restroom and buy a snack, and maybe some coffee too.

I exited the car. "Do you want anything from inside?"

He flashed me that annoying smile. "I'm good, sweetheart."

And we were back to that.

I rolled my eyes. If I was to spend the next few days with him, we would need to have a serious conversation about this sweetheart thing.

Thankfully, the restroom in this gas station was large and clean. I did my business, then stopped by the front where I picked up a bottle of water, a cup of fresh coffee, and a small packet of Oreos. I paid for it in cash and exited the convenience store.

Leviathan had finished filling up the car and parked it in front of the entrance. I reached for the car's door when a tingling sensation traveled through my back.

Oh, no.

I glanced around, my eyes wide. Where were they? How had they found me?

Shit, I skipped a dose of my potion, hadn't I? That was plausible.

Leviathan lowered the window. "Don't you want to get going, sweetheart? Get in the car."

"Right." I opened the door, intent on keeping it cool.

I didn't get the chance.

Rays of light hit the ground at my feet, and I jumped. The drinks and the snacks fell from my arms as people screamed and ran ... and angels walked into the gas station.

I froze in place, watching them.

White wings out, folded behind their backs, in golden and white uniform, and their Celestial Swords in hand.

A pang cut through my heart.

I recovered once they stopped.

Julien pointed his sword at me. "We've been looking for you."

Leviathan exited the car. "What's going on?"

"Mind your own business, demon," Izrail said. There were three more, the same ones who had been in Houston, but I certainly hadn't met the other two. They looked young, probably recently graduated from the academy, and with their heads filled with lies about me.

Leviathan rounded the car and stood a couple of feet to my side. "She's my business."

Julien snickered. "You really are associating with demons now."

"Not now," another angel said. "Since the attack."

"Before that," Izrail said. "It had to be before that."

"You don't know what you're talking about," I said, a threat in my tone.

"We don't?" Julien took a step forward. "Then come with us. Plead your case. Tell us what we don't know."

I could go with them. That was the right thing to do. I was innocent. By running, I was only making it worse. But if I went, I knew it was over. Rhodes would find a way to kill me. I couldn't find out what was going on and clear my name.

I held my ground. "I can't."

Julien snarled. "You've asked for it."

They sent bolts of light magic toward me. I jumped out of range. Leviathan moved to the other side while throwing darkfire at the angels.

Part of me wanted to tell him to stop. To not hurt them. But what were we supposed to do? We had to get out of here!

I hid behind a gas pump, my heart beating a million miles per hour. I could see humans cowering behind the store's windows, and around its corner. Some of them had their phones out and were recording this.

I didn't understand. Angels were never this careless. We always avoided being seen, being found out.

That showed me how desperate they were to get me.

These humans would receive a visit from the memory fairy, who would also erase all of their electronics and scrape the internet.

I glanced around the pump and saw Julien prepare a light bolt and throw it at the pump at my back!

I ran. Three steps in, I saw a young woman cowering behind her car, right beside the pump. I skidded to change my course, grabbed her arm hard, and pulled her with me.

The pump exploded in a cloud of fire. The woman and I fell forward into a flowerbed at the gas station's lot limit. I slammed my knees pretty hard and groaned.

The woman looked back and let out a cry. Her car was turned over, engulfed by flames.

"Thank you," she muttered, her voice breaking.

"Just run," I told her.

With wobbly legs, she shot up and ran to the side.

The heat of the fire licking at me, I stood and looked at the scene. Half of the gas station was on fire, the ceiling caved in, the windows of the store broken, a few humans bleeding.

It was one thing to come and do things in front of humans, knowing they could later erase their memories, and another to put humans at risk on purpose!

What the hell?

Distracted by the fire, I didn't see Julien rushed me. He grabbed me from behind. He wrapped his arm around my middle and raised his sword to my neck. On instinct, I grabbed his sword to push it away, threw myself forward, making him lose his balance and his grip around me. As I twisted out of his grip, he swept his sword and cut my upper arm.

I groaned in pain.

I tried turning and running, but my head felt fuzzy, my legs heavy. What the hell?

Julien grabbed my wrists and kept me close, his sword pointed at my face. "There's nowhere to run."

"I'm not going to stop running!" I yelled. "Until I can prove I'm innocent, I won't stop!"

"If you're innocent, then come with me."

"The moment I set foot in Elysium, I'm dead." Or not. I knew Rhodes wanted something from me. He would kill me only after he got it.

He pushed the blade closer to my throat. "Don't make me use this."

I knew he wouldn't let me go. I knew he would use the sword. They would do anything to catch me, I knew that now.

I pulled on my arm with everything I had. Julien clambered forward. I snatched his sword as he tried recovering his balance before he kissed the ground, turned it around, and slammed the hilt against his temple.

He fell on the ground, unconscious.

When I looked up, the other angels were running toward me.

Oh, shit.

The sound of wheels screeching reached my ears. Leviathan lowered the window of the car, threw a wave of darkfire toward the angels, making them cower, and stopped the car right beside me.

I opened the door, jumped in, and he peeled off before my feet were fully inside.

8

———

LEVIATHAN KEPT GLANCING AT ME, MAKING ME FEEL WEIRD.

Finally, he asked. "What was that?"

Where was the flirty tone when you needed it? Ugh.

"It's none of your business." I reached into my bag and grabbed the damn potion. Yup, I had forgotten the last dose and I was now paying for it.

I drank it, knowing it would instantly cut off my aura and the angels wouldn't be able to find me.

For now.

"Angels were after you, sweetheart. They came after me. That is my business. What did you do? Steal something from them? A magical book? A powerful weapon?"

I glared at him. "Just shut it." The sting in my arm increased and I bit my tongue not to cry out.

"You're hurt," Leviathan said, casting more glances my way. It wasn't a question.

"I'm fine," I said, my voice shaking. "It'll heal." It hurt like hell, and if he could feel that, then great.

He had fought alongside me just now, no questions asked.

It was probably the bond and the fact that if they hurt me, he would hurt too, but that was okay.

At least both of us had escaped.

Now, if only I had something for the pain.

"Sweetheart, how bad is it?"

"Not bad, it just stings." I settled low on the seat, resting my head back. The fight must have exhausted my stamina, because suddenly, all I wanted was to sleep. "I'll close my eyes for a moment …"

I could have sworn I had blinked, but suddenly, Leviathan was on the other side of the car, picking me up in his arms.

"Shit, sweetheart," he muttered. "This doesn't look good."

I opened my mouth to interject, but my tongue was heavy, and I couldn't speak. My head swam and it hurt when Leviathan moved me, taking the steps to … somewhere.

I couldn't keep my eyes open, but I got a peek of a shoddy staircase and a door with some random number. Then Leviathan deposited me on a soft mattress.

"Let me take a look, sweetheart." He reached for me and stripped off my jacket. A string of curses flew from his lips. "I can feel the pain, Ariella, but this is much worse than I thought."

"I …" I tried speaking. I didn't even know what I would say.

Ignoring him, I turned on my side, and curled into a ball. My body shook, my arm throbbed, but I was too tired to do anything about it. All I wanted was to sleep.

"I need help," Leviathan said. When I peeked again, he was on the phone. "Use one of your coins and open a portal. Now or she'll die, and I'll die with her!"

He lowered the phone, extended his right hand, and closed his eyes. A moment later, a shimmering black light formed around his fingertips. It grew and spread, forming a thin, oval veil.

A woman stepped through it.

The veil poofed away and the woman hovered over me. "What happened?" she asked.

I tried asking her who she was, what she was doing, tell her that I didn't like strangers touching me, but no words came out. Only some grunts and groans, and then a scream when the pain suddenly stung too much.

"She was attacked by angels," Leviathan said through gritted teeth. "I think the blade they use to cut her was poisoned."

The woman stuck her finger on my wound and I screamed again. She then took her finger to her mouth and licked it. "It is poison, but I believe it was to make her lose consciousness, to immobilize, not to kill."

"They wanted her alive, not dead," Leviathan observed. The woman nodded. "Can you do something about it?"

She offered him a smug half-grin. Where had I seen that before. "You wouldn't have called me if you thought I couldn't."

The woman pressed her hand on top of my wound, closed her eyes, and started humming. Dark red and black lights shone from between her palm and my skin. At first, the sting hurt more and I even heard Leviathan's grunt as he endured the pain. I was too far gone to care.

But as she healed me, I felt more aware, more awake, and the pain stung like a bitch. Smoke drifted away from her hand to the ceiling.

"That's the poison," she said. "Now we need to heal this cut." A dark red light shone and I could feel my skin stretching and closing.

I bit down on my tongue not to scream.

Suddenly, too aware, I sat up.

"Easy there, sweetheart," Leviathan said. I glanced at him, seated beside me on the bed. He looked terrible.

I stared at the woman standing beside the bed. She was a lot younger than I first thought. "You're healing me."

She nodded. "I'm not done yet." She showed me her hands. "May I?"

I hesitated. Before, I had been barely conscious, but now? Should I trust her? Well, if she or Leviathan wanted me dead, they had missed a fantastic opportunity.

I glanced at my arm—my skin was bloody, so was my jacket and the bedsheets. Even Levi's hands were smeared with my blood, but there was only a thick, red line cutting the side of my bicep, a good three inches.

I nodded.

She rested a hand over the wound and infused it with more of her magic. "I don't think I'll be able to make it disappear completely, but it'll look like an old, thin scar."

She stared at me with bright blue eyes. I knew these. They looked just like Leviathan's. I glanced between them. The woman had the same black hair, but she wore it long, to the middle of her back, the same fair skin, the same straight nose.

"You're related," I said.

"I'm Lacey, Levi's little sister."

"Levi?" I asked.

"Yeah, it's what I call him." She leaned closer and half whispered, "He doesn't really like it, not since we were kids. I call him that mostly to irritate him."

"Maybe I should call him that too," I joked. He irritated me with sweetheart. Now it was my turn.

"You definitely should," she said with a small smile. "Now, I'm almost done. Once I take my magic away, the adrenaline will fade almost instantly and the exhaustion will win. Don't fight it. You need to rest to completely heal."

I didn't like the idea of passing out with two strangers, but why go through all the trouble of healing me if they wanted to kill me? It made no sense.

True to her word, Lacey withdrew her hand and a wave of dizziness fell over me. I felt the bed sway under me, and a big hand cradle my head to the pillows.

I blinked, fighting it, but there was no winning.

"Rest, sweetheart," was the last thing I heard before drifting to sleep.

***

"I SHOULDN'T HAVE TOLD YOU."

"No, I'm glad you did, Levi ... even if it took hours to make you spill."

I came to and recognized Leviathan and Lacey's voices. I peeked from under my lashes, but all I saw was the heavy curtain over the window and faint light streaming from underneath. Was it still the same afternoon, or the next morning?

Leviathan groaned. "You're so annoying."

"If I were, you wouldn't care," Lacey said.

They were somewhere behind me. I kept my breathing slow, lest they knew I had woken up. For some reason, I didn't want them to know yet.

"All right then. You're my favorite sister."

"I'm the only one you have!"

"That we know of. Do you really believe father doesn't

have offspring out in the wild? Most higher demons can't keep their junk in their pants."

"You can."

He scoffed. "I don't, actually. I'm just careful not to get anyone pregnant. Can you imagine me as a father? I'll be worse than our old man."

A pause. "I doubt that."

"Enough." Leviathan sounded upset. "About this damn bond, can you break it?"

Shit, he was trying to get rid of me. If he did, he probably wouldn't help me get my wings back. I could always call my friends, I knew that, but I felt so embarrassed. They were all powerful, and I was nothing more than an ordinary human now.

No, I would rather a stranger see this side of me.

Another pause. "With my magic, I can feel the bond. Just a faint string pulling you to her."

"It's anything but faint. Can you break it?" he asked again, his tone impatient.

"I think so, but I will take a proper ritual," Lacey said. "I would have to go back to the coven and prepare and—"

I stirred then, interrupting their conversation. If she was going to explain to him how to get rid of me, I would rather he didn't hear it.

I turned in bed, with a fake yawn, and faced them. Levi and Lacey were seated on the second bed, a bag from Dunkin' Donuts among them.

"Good morning, sweetheart," Leviathan said, flipping the charming switch. "Hope you had a good night's sleep."

I sat up and rubbed my eyes. "Is it morning?"

Lacey nodded. "We took turns watching over you, but I think you're all healed."

I looked at my arm. A thin, barely-there line cut across the side of my biceps, looking more like an old scar than a recent poisoned wound.

"Thank you," I told her.

"Don't thank me." She smiled. "Thank this knucklehead. If Levi had taken another ten minutes to call me, I'm not sure I could have extracted the poison and reversed its effects."

I looked at Leviathan. He stared at me for a second, and when I opened my mouth to thank him, he cut me off. "Here." He lowered his to-go coffee cup, grabbed another one from the nightstand and offered it to me. "You like black coffee, don't you, sweetheart?"

I almost cringed at the sweetheart thing. He had been so serious talking to Lacey just now, and before when he was saving me, and yet, he was right back to being a charming jerk.

I took the cup from him. "Thanks, *Levi*, but I prefer it with plenty of sugar."

Leviathan narrowed his eyes at me, visibly irritated. "Don't call me that."

"Why? Does it bother you? Then don't call me sweetheart."

"I'll call you what I want, sweetheart."

"Then get used to it, Levi."

He groaned, and stifling a chuckle, Lacey cut him off before he could say anything else. "I have sweetener." She lifted a couple of packets from inside the bag.

"That will work." I got them from her.

A tense silence stretched between us while I drank my coffee, got one of the donuts from the bag, and we finished our breakfast. Thankfully, they didn't ask about the angels and why they were after me, and since I didn't want to answer anything, it was only fair I didn't ask anything either.

Even though I wanted to ask a lot of things.

Who was their father? Was he as bad as they made him sound? I mean, they mentioned he was a higher demon, like Leviathan—no, *Levi*—and all demons were terrible, but maybe evil beings weren't so evil to their children?

I remembered something about a coin and portal and ...

All right, there was something I wanted to know. "So, you're a witch?"

Lacey took a sip of her coffee and nodded. "Half demon, half witch."

"What coven?"

"A very old, and reclusive coven that doesn't like to get mixed up with the rest of the supernatural world."

I frowned. "But here you are, helping an angel."

"Well, they don't need to know everything I do, or don't do." She winked at me, flashing me a wide, bright smile. Damn, she was as beautiful as her brother. Seeing the two side-by-side was unsettling.

The fact that she didn't tell me which coven she was from didn't escape me. These reclusive witches didn't want to be found.

"I don't think I've heard of many witches with healing gifts," I said.

"It's rare, especially in my coven," she said, looking uncomfortable. Averting her gaze, she stood and threw her empty cup in the trash can under the desk. "So, what's the plan now?"

"You're going back to your coven, and we'll continue our road trip." Levi stood up too and grabbed the empty food packets from the bed.

"I left a letter to my mentor. I told her I won't be back for a few days. I can tag along for now."

Levi shook his head. "No way in hell."

I frowned. What was so bad about her joining us? A half demon, half witch going after my wings with us? Another magical being on our side. Because, really, with me so powerless, our odds of defeating whoever was holding my wings was meager.

I stood. "Why not? You should come."

Lacey beamed, looking younger. If I was twenty-three, Levi looked like twenty-seven, maybe twenty-eight, she had to be nineteen, at most. I had been through a lot by the time I was nineteen, and I knew many impressive fae, witches, and whatnot who at nineteen led supernaturals through war.

I glanced from a happy Lacey to a miserable Levi. His hands were clean, and his clothes crisp. I was sure he had taken a shower and changed sometime during the night.

I wanted to be clean too.

I found my duffel bag on the desk. "But before we go, I want a shower and to change into clean clothes."

9

"The angels have seen it," Levi said as he used his phone to rent a different car. "Plus, my Ferrari is a two-seater. We wouldn't all fit in it."

So, he left his Ferrari behind at the inn, where according to him, his demons would come to pick it up, and we got a Range Rover from the nearest rental place.

Lacey used her magic to make the guy forget we were there and that we had rented the car. If the angels came looking, they would see the car had been rented by an old guy to take his family for a road trip along the east coast.

On the other side of the country from our destination.

Once we were settled in the car—Levi driving, me in the passenger seat, though I had insisted on sitting in the back, and Lacey behind her brother—I grabbed the small vial of potion and drank half a dose.

The damn thing was almost empty and this trip was already taking longer than I had expected.

"Shit," I muttered under my breath.

"What?" Lacey scooted closer to the front seat.

"This potion." I showed her the almost empty vial. Levi glanced at it for half a second before returning his attention to the road. I sighed. "Ever since I lost my magic, the angels have been able to see my aura and find me. Thankfully, I found a witch who could make me potions to act as an aura suppressant. But the main ingredient, Mage Bloom, is rare and expensive and she hasn't been able to get enough of it."

"That's why they found you at the gas station," Levi said.

I nodded. "And I'm running out now. Unless you have a stash of Mage Bloom lying around and can find a witch who is versed in potions, we'll deal with more angels until I find my wings."

Until I got my magic back, actually. My wings were a missing limb and I desperately missed them but recovering them wouldn't do much for me other than make me feel like an angel again. And allow me entrance to Elysium again.

"Actually, I know a witch who might have this plant." Lacey leaned back in her seat and grabbed her phone.

"What?" I twisted in my seat to look at her.

She pressed a couple of buttons then put her phone to her ear. "Hi, it's me. Yeah, I know. Listen, do you have Mage Bloom?" Her face fell. "No? Damn it. We really need it." Her eyes met mine. "But you can get it. A lot of it? Then get it. We're coming your way." Beside me, Levi groaned. "Yeah, me, Levi, and a friend. All right. I'll let you know when we arrive. Bye."

"What happened?" I asked. I mean, I had heard it, but I needed confirmation.

"I found you a witch who can get Mage Bloom, and she's talented with potions," Lacey said, sounding proud. "If you know what else goes in the potions, or the gist of it, I'm sure she can do it."

She had mentioned having a lot of Mage Bloom, and unless Sylvie was abusing me and my desperation, this plant was expensive. But I wouldn't say no to this, even if I had to get there, buy the quantity I could pay for, and arrange to buy the rest later.

"That's amazing. Thank you."

Lacey shrugged and leaned over Levi's seat again. "We have to change course."

He met her eyes through the rearview mirror, fuming again. "You didn't even ask me. I'm not willing to go there. It'll add two days to this fucking trip."

My shoulders sagged. Two more days?

"But you heard what Ariella said," Lacey countered. "If she doesn't have more of the potion soon, the angels are going to find her. Do you prefer adding two days of boring travel or dealing with a handful, maybe a dozen angels by ourselves? I know you're powerful, but I doubt you can take a dozen angels, especially high-ranked ones, by yourself."

Levi glanced at me, and for a moment, I thought he would strangle me. "This wasn't part of your wish, sweetheart. I expect some kind of payment for this."

Shit. "I'll figure something out."

Though we had left yesterday, we hadn't gone far because of my wound. We were about thirty minutes north of Dallas, which meant, we still had a twenty-four-hour drive to San Francisco.

Levi reached to the car screen and pressed a couple of buttons, changing our destination to Durango, Colorado— about seven hours northwest. "I hope you have a thicker jacket, sweetheart."

Damn, Colorado in February was a lot colder than Houston, but from the map, I could see it was on the southern border, so maybe it wasn't so bad.

Without anything else to do for that long, I leaned back in my seat and tried to sleep.

Try being the important word of that sentence.

Despite yesterday's fight, I was wound up and couldn't shut off my brain.

The angels had found me again.

Had they erased the humans' memories already? I opened the browser on my phone and searched for news about the gas station. I found some, but all the articles mentioned a freaky accident where a pump exploded and they didn't know why. A few humans were hurt, but nothing critical.

Yup, they had done their homework already.

What would they do the next time they found me? Because they would find me again unless I could get plenty of potions.

How would I pay this witch? I had only a couple thousand dollars left. I would need to go back to Houston and fight three times per week, if not more, to pay for it.

But I couldn't do that and retrieve my wings. I hoped this witch accepted what I had. Maybe I could find a fight club in Durango and earn some money.

Hm, not sure I liked the idea of fighting with Levi and Lacey around.

Maybe I could rob a bank.

I sighed.

A long time ago, that thought would never have crossed my mind, but I had been on Earth for so long, and around so many supernaturals and humans with their complicated feelings and actions, it was rubbing off on me.

I didn't like it.

"Pretending to sleep, hm, sweetheart?"

I fixed my seat and looked at Levi. "I know you'll say no, but I mean it: If you get tired, I can drive."

"I like driving, sweetheart. It gives me time to think."

I forced a gasp. "Demons think?"

"Ha-ha-ha." He spared me a quick glance. "Are all angels this funny?"

He was teasing me, because I knew that hadn't been funny at all. I heard a soft breathing and looked back. Lacey was turned sideways in the backseat, sleeping with her back to the door.

If only I could sleep like that.

Not even after a fight did I sleep like that.

I folded one leg under me and twisted my body so I was half-turned to Levi. "So, you have a sister."

He glanced at me again. "I only do small talk if I have something to gain, sweetheart, and what I could want from you, I doubt you'll give me."

My brows knotted down. "How do you know if you haven't asked?"

Levi shook his head. "There's no reason to complicate things, sweetheart."

I groaned. "Can we stop with this sweetheart thing at least."

He flashed me that half grin. "Why, sweetheart?"

I rolled my eyes. "You probably use that on all women who fall into your bed, and hell, I'm not like those women."

"One, you don't know the kind of women I take to bed, and two, see, I told you you wouldn't give it to me."

I stared at him, my jaw slack. Was it sex he wanted from me? In exchange for small talk, he wanted to sleep with me?

His statement appalled me, but a sliver of pride filled my core. He found me attractive. I mean, I hoped he was the kind of guy to only sleep with women he found attractive, right? Or at least hot enough to bed.

I shook my head, clearing my mind of such thoughts.

"Seriously, stop calling me that," I said.

"Will you stop calling me Levi?"

"Not a chance."

"Then get used to it, sweetheart."

I stared at his perfect profile for a moment. "Why don't you like us to call you Levi?"

"I don't do small talk, remember?"

"You're impossible."

"I've heard worse." He adjusted his grip on the wheel, barely touching it. "I'll say this, though: You know Levi bothers me, and that's why you're calling me that. It's the same for me. The more I see it bothers you, the more I'll do it." He stared at me for a long time. "Sweetheart?"

I punched his arm. "Pay attention to the road!"

"This car practically drives itself. All I need to do is keep my hands on the wheel."

"Still!"

With a small chuckle, Levi moved a little on the seat, and focused on the road.

This wasn't good.

Here I was in a car with two half-higher demons and joking with one. Or whatever this was.

I knew the world wasn't as black and white as they had taught us at the Guardian Academy. I had lived in it a long time now to be friends with all kinds of supernaturals, even to know and respect other half demons.

But this felt different. It was like Levi, Lacey, and I had

suddenly formed our own gang and it was us against the world. Or rather, us unified in my mission: to buy more potion and get my wings.

It all kept changing. I went to Levi to get my wings and magic back. If I found the higher demon who had taken my wings in the process, great.

Hazel and I accidentally bound Levi to me, and then he told me he couldn't get my magic back. My wings and revenge on Molraz were already a lot better than nothing.

Now, we were running from the angels who had found me, and going to see a witch who supposedly could make more potion for me.

What else could happen?

Maybe I would find another dragon in some random mountain when we stopped for gas and we would need to save it from evil supernaturals who only wanted its power—it had happened before!

We drove in almost completely silence for the next two hours. Lacey woke up and tried to talk to Levi, but he shut her down. Around one in the afternoon, we decided it was time for gas and lunch. Levi stopped the car beside a diner across the street from a gas station and told us to start ordering while he filled up the tank.

Lacey and I got a booth by the windows, from where we could see Levi. It was already a little colder here and I was glad for the heating in the diner.

The server came up to us the moment we sat down, and we ordered three burgers with fries and sweet tea. When she walked away, I glanced at Levi again.

Dressed in slacks, a button-down shirt, and an open jacket, so crisp and sharp, beside that fancy SUV, he looked like a millionaire entrepreneur on important business.

Not a demon.

Oh, I was sure he was a millionaire, if not a billionaire, but if I had walked by him in Houston, I would never have guessed who he really was and what he could do.

Lacey cleared her throat and I snapped my head to her. "So, how did you get mixed up with my brother?"

I almost laughed. "Didn't he tell you while I was unconscious?"

"He told me you summoned him and bound him to you so he would grant your wishes."

My mouth fell open. "That makes it sound so bad."

"Oh, don't worry, I know it isn't. Levi is either way too charming for his own good, or too cold and stoic. He gives an abridged version of any situation and usually from his point of view."

That did sound like him.

For some reason, Lacey didn't feel like a demon to me. She was much more like a witch, and I could deal with that. I had plenty of witch friends and I liked them all.

So, I told her the truth. About having lost my wings, my sword, and later my powers—though I didn't go in detail how—about having to flee from the angels—again, didn't explain why—and how I needed a potion to hide my aura. I also told her about the witch who made the potion for me and the lack of Mage Bloom.

"I got desperate," I told her. "I went to your brother to ask for my wings and magic back, but his price was too high. When I talked to the witch, she told me the prices have gone up even more. I didn't think twice." I had actually thought twice, thrice, four times. "I asked a friend to help me summon him. He would grant my wishes, and in return, I would free him from the summoning circle. That would be the price. But something in the spell went wrong and Levi ended up tied to me."

"Summoning spells aren't easy, and Levi is a strong higher demon. He must have fought it like hell."

I nodded. "I feel bad about putting him in this position, but I don't regret it. I want my wings back. I need them."

What kind of angel didn't have wings? Though my magic was what would protect me from the angels, I wanted my wings more.

"I understand. I would probably do the same thing." She glanced at her hands. "I can't imagine not having what makes me a witch." Her blue eyes softened. "I'm sorry."

I nodded, and changed subjects since I wasn't great at talking about my problems and feelings. "Have you and Levi always gotten along?"

"In a way," she said, her tone turning sad. "Levi and I lost our mothers when we were young, so our father took us in. But he was never there. As a higher demon, he's as bad as you can make them, and he was like that with us. He didn't have patience with us, and he was always yelling and punishing us for the silliest things." She shook her head. "At least, that's how I remember it."

"That doesn't sound good."

"It wasn't bad, though, because he was almost always gone, so it was Levi and me for a while. We had nannies and housekeepers, but they never lasted. When my magic manifested at nine, our father said it reminded him of my mother, and he loathed her. So, Levi suggested he send me to my mother's coven. The witches would welcome me and raise me as their own. And that's exactly what he did."

"Levi stayed back. Alone."

She nodded. "I tried to go to him. Once, I succeeded, and

my father was home. Whatever his deal had been that day, it hadn't work. In fact, I think it had gone terribly wrong because he took out his rage on me."

I pressed a hand to my mouth. "No!"

"Levi saved me. He was seventeen at the time, almost as tall as our father and just as powerful. He fought our father, rescued me, sent me back to the coven, and told me to never come back." Her eyes filled with tears. "Right after, Levi abandoned our father and started living by himself. Then, he allowed me to visit a couple of times each year. Our relationship isn't what we both would like, but I know he cares a lot about me, and I care about him."

"I know what you mean." I had never told this to any of my friends on Earth, but I had a sister back home, and I would do anything for her.

I glanced at the window again. Levi was parking the SUV in front of the diner. It was hard to reconcile the image I had of Levi with the picture Lacey painted.

"Please, don't tell him I told you all of this," she said quickly. "He always says I talk too much, and no one should know the truth about us."

"I won't say anything."

Relief flooded her features.

Levi slipped into the seat beside Lacey five seconds before the server came with our food. Even though she could be his mother, or at least a young aunt, she batted her fake lashes at Levi and asked if he wanted anything else.

He didn't even look in her direction. "No, thanks." But then he stared at Lacey and me. "Eat fast, go to the restroom, and let's go. We shouldn't stay in one spot for long, and we have a long road ahead of us."

"Yes, boss," Lacey teased.

Levi ignored her and took a bite of his cheeseburger.

"Lacey, how did you get here? Were you close by?" I asked before taking a bite of my food.

"No, Levi used one of the golden coins we spelled." He glared at her and she shrank down. "Sorry."

He shook his head. "Always saying more than you should."

"Hey, stop bothering her," I protested. "If you're afraid people will know how you get around, don't worry, I won't tell anyone."

Levi stared at me for five seconds before saying, "The coins work one way, to portal her to me. That's all."

That made sense. Portaling was a difficult spell and using tokens to help out was a nice touch.

Levi munched on his food fast and furious. In less than three minutes, he was almost done with his burger. He took the final bite and stiffened.

I followed his gaze. On the other side of the diner, our server talked to another one, a young brunette.

"What is it?" I asked.

"Shhh," was all he said. We stayed in silence for a few seconds. "Fuck. They are talking about you."

"What? Why? What are they saying?"

"That you're the missing girl a group was inquiring about a couple of hours earlier." I froze. He went on, "Apparently, the angels came this way and pretended to be looking for their missing friend. They gave a good description of you and me, the kidnapper."

"Oh, shit," I muttered.

"We better go before they call the cops, or worse, the angels." Levi shot up.

I grabbed the rest of my fries, Lacey grabbed her drink, and we all bolted out of the diner.

"Wait!" the young waitress called out, racing after us.

We didn't stop. She grabbed her phone from her apron pocket and started calling someone.

We piled into the SUV and Levi peeled out of the parking lot, going as fast as the car could go.

10

Meanwhile, we talked about possible scenarios for what happened and the one that made the most sense was that after bumping into us at the gas station outside of Houston, the angels fanned out to search for us—for me. They stopped wherever they could, asking about me, and to not look like weirdos, they created this story about their missing friend.

"When we get to Heidi, she and I can create a ward around the house, something to mute our auras," Lacey suggested. "It won't have the same effect as the potion, but it could buy us some time while she makes it."

Because of Levi's heavy foot, we cut the trip by almost thirty minutes and arrived in Durango a little after four. There was a thin layer of snow accumulated on lawns, but the road was clean, as if it hadn't snowed in a few days.

Levi steered the car into a rural neighborhood, and after a few minutes, pulled the SUV into a short driveway. I glanced at the house, bathed in sunlight, and could see a witch living in there—maybe even a Halliwell from Charmed. It was a narrow three-story Victorian, with brown siding and white accents. The snow-covered front garden had a thick tree in the center and a few shrubs that acted like a fence.

As we exited the car, the front door opened, and a woman in a bright pink sweaterdress walked out.

"Lacey! Levi!" the woman exclaimed, opening her arms.

"It's so good to see you." Lacey raced to her and gave her a bear hug, while Levi raised his hand and greeted her from afar.

She let him be and then looked at me.

I tensed a bit. Heidi was a short woman in her sixties (or so, I thought. Nowadays, it was too hard to guess people's ages, especially a witch, who lived a lot longer than humans) with luscious brown hair, plump arms, and a warm smile. Her hazel eyes shone with contentment, even though we had brought trouble to her doorstep.

"Hi, there, I'm Heidi." She offered me her hand.

"Ariella." I slipped my hand in hers. "Nice to meet you."

She gripped my hand tight, and I could feel her magic around me. Her smile widened and she let go of my hand. "You have a good heart." She gestured to Lacey and Levi. "Just like those two."

Levi shook his head and walked into the house.

Lacey gave her a "really?" look. "You know he doesn't like it when you say that. Or that you tell others. He's supposed to be an evil higher demon."

"Well, he certainly acts like one most of the time," Heidi said. "And yes, his heart is darker, but ultimately, it's still a good one."

I frowned, considering this information. That, added to the fact that Levi had protected Lacey from their wicked father, I didn't know what to do with it.

I let it slip from my mind. It was better if I believed Levi was the evil demon he wanted to be.

"Let's get out of the cold, Ariella." Heidi guided us to the door. "Tell me what you need."

"First, we need to do something," Lacey said. She explained about the ward to mute auras.

"We can do that." Heidi pointed to the door. "Go in, Ariella, feel at home. The restroom is under the stairs and there's food in the kitchen."

I nodded and disappeared past the door, rubbing my cold hands together, while the two witches walked to the road in front of the house.

The door opened to a small foyer with stairs to the second floor, and beside it a hallway that led to the back. On one side was the living room and the other the dining room—all heavily decorated but comfortable looking, showing that someone really lived here. I stopped by the bathroom, then headed to the back, where the kitchen was.

Levi was there, grabbing a beer from the fridge. I glanced around. Lots of small appliances sat on top of the black counters along with some weird pieces, like the yellow metal chicken where the eggs were placed, and the ceramic open watermelon for the fruit. On the side was a tall counter with stools that separated it from the dining room, and on the opposite side was a bay window overlooking the backyard with bench seats and a wooden table.

I did a double take at the backyard—it was snowless, the grass so green and lush and full of colorful flowers.

Levi followed my gaze. "It's enchanted. Heidi doesn't like the cold, so she keeps the interior and the back of her house in a perpetual spring."

That was amazing. She probably kept the front with snow

so the neighbors or anyone who drove by didn't become suspicious.

The entire house was quaint and old and with lots of character. "I like it," I said.

"Want something to drink, sweetheart?" Levi held the fridge open.

"Water, please."

He closed the fridge, grabbed a glass cup from one of the cabinets—he knew where it was located—and filled it with water from the fridge's water dispenser. He handed it to me.

"Thanks."

He leaned back on the counter and took a sip of his beer. "What Heidi said ... she doesn't know what she's talking about."

"Doesn't she use magic to sense that?"

"She does, but I think she feels a sliver of good in the middle of my black heart and she holds on to that with both hands, as if she could will it to grow." He scoffed and took another sip. "It would be easier for hell to freeze over."

I didn't want to get involved, but I couldn't help my curiosity. "How do you know her?"

He offered me his trademark lopsided grin. "Wouldn't you like to know, sweetheart? Remember, I don't do small talk. We're here to get your potion and then we're leaving."

Without looking at me again, Levi walked out the door to the porch in the backyard. I could see him from the bay window but chose to turn my back to him.

Who cared how Levi and Lacey knew Heidi? Who cared if Levi had the potential to be good? As long as I got my potion, I surely didn't.

I found a casserole on the range and was about to lift the

aluminum foil that covered it to find out what it was when Lacey and Heidi entered the kitchen.

"It's done," Lacey announced. "I would say the angels can't find us for the next twenty-four hours."

"That should be enough time to make a potion," Heidi said. "Unless it's more complicated than it seems." She extended her hand to me. "Can I see it?"

I grabbed the small vial from my pocket and handed it to her. She brought it up against the kitchen's light and looked at it. "Hm, I need to go to my shed, find out what is in here, and then make my own."

She started for the back door and Lacey followed.

"Wait," I said. "About payment ... I don't have a lot of money. I might be able to pay you half now—"

"Who said anything about payment?" Heidi cut me off.

"But this potion costs a lot back home. I thought—"

"Nonsense, girl. I'll make as much as I can and it's a gift."

"But ..." I closed my mouth. This felt wrong, and at the same, I couldn't deny this was perfect. If I didn't have to pay, it would make a lot of things easier. "I feel like I'm taking advantage of you."

She smiled at me reassuringly. "You're not, Ariella. I'm doing this because I want to." She exited to the porch and Lacey went with her.

I followed them.

We passed Levi, seated on the wicker bench on the porch, and took a stone path to a large shed several yards away from the house.

"Welcome to my shed," Heidi said, opening the doors wide.

I glanced around, amazed. It reminded me of Sylvie's

workplace, and also of Khalisa's store and back room, but it was even more crammed and lively.

Shelves lined the walls, filled with all kinds of plants and ingredients, and a large wooden table took up the remaining space. It was piled high with books, mortars and pestles, a heating element, and there were even boxes underneath it. Two empty cauldrons stood on the left side, near a small window.

Heidi rounded the table. "I'll probably need to use most of this to find out what is in it. Is that okay?"

Shit. What if she used it and then found out she didn't have the other ingredients? Or that she couldn't do it?

I let out a long breath. "Sure."

She tipped the vial and let three drops fall in a white bowl. She took the bowl to the heating element. After a few seconds, an acrid scent filled the space and even the open doors didn't help. The liquid bubbled with the heat, and suddenly, it parted in seven.

Heidi lowered her head and took a big whiff. "Oh, I have everything."

Relief washed through me. "That's good."

She smiled at me as she grabbed a blue cloth from under the table. She placed it on the table and unfolded the cloth, revealing the Mage Bloom. "And here's the main ingredient."

"Was it hard to get it?" I asked, worried it would cost me a fortune.

"Hard? No, not really," Heidi said. "It isn't a common plant, but if you know where to look, you'll find plenty."

I frowned. Sylvie said it was a rare plant, expensive, and her supplier couldn't get more. She had even contacted other witches. Unless she, her supplier, and the other witches had really bad contacts, this didn't make sense.

Lacey took off her jacket. "Should we start, then?"

Heidi nodded. "It'll take us a couple of hours to prepare the ingredients, and then another handful of hours for the potion to brew. You should go back to the house, Ariella. Rest, watch TV, eat. Oh, there are two guest bedrooms upstairs, and they are ready for you."

"You and I can stay in the one with two single beds," Lacey said. "Levi can take the other one."

My shoulders sagged. I kinda guessed we would be here for a while, but it seemed we would have to sleep here and the potion wouldn't be ready until next morning.

I really hoped the ward around the house held.

"Can I help in any way?" I asked. I had no idea what it entailed, but they could give me directions. Anything to make it go faster.

Heidi leaned closer and half whispered, "Four hands is already too many, but I know Lacey won't let me shoo her away."

"Damn straight," Lacey said, bobbing her head once.

As if I wasn't there anymore, the pair turned to each other and started working like a well-oiled machine.

Slowly, I retreated.

Levi was still on the bench on the porch, his beer empty on the table beside him, and his phone pressed to his ear.

"I know," he said. "But you better have it done by the time I come back."

He didn't look at me as I walked by, and I didn't look at him. His words faded as I entered the kitchen and closed the door behind me.

I glanced around the kitchen as I had done before and my eyes found the casserole on the range. Should I eat? I was a little hungry and the witches had mentioned it would take them a couple of hours to prepare the potion.

There was Levi, but I wouldn't ask him.

I opened the cabinets, looking for plates, cups, and utensils. When I had grabbed one of each, Levi entered the kitchen.

"What are you doing, sweetheart?" His gaze found the plate and utensils beside the range, and the casserole. "Look, Heidi is great at potions, but horrible at cooking. Whatever that is, it probably tastes like cardboard. I'm not eating that."

I shrugged. "Then don't."

"Come on." He started for the hallway.

"What?"

"There used to be an Italian restaurant not far from here. Let's go, sweetheart."

"I can't." I gestured to the house. "Heidi and Lacey warded the house. I shouldn't leave."

"Right." He raised a finger. "I'll be right back."

He walked outside to the shed. He disappeared inside it for a couple of minutes, then he came back, holding a necklace with a thin silver chain and a small circular pendant.

"What is that?"

"Heidi put the same ward on the necklace. It should hold for a couple of hours."

I reached for it, stunned. "Just for a couple of hours? Couldn't she do it permanently?"

It would be amazing to wear a necklace that could hide my aura, instead of drinking a potion every couple of days.

Levi tsked. "If she could, I'm sure she would have told us, sweetheart." He gestured to the door. "Coming or not?"

11

———

LEVI DROVE US TO THE HEART OF THE NEIGHBORHOOD AND parked the car at a strip shopping center, a few spots from the Italian restaurant. We barely said anything as we ordered our food and ate—a shrimp alfredo pasta for me, and fettuccine with steak in red wine sauce for Levi.

We had also ordered a lasagna to take back, so Lacey and Heidi would have dinner once they were done with the potion.

Levi carried the paper bag, and, when we exited, I headed to the car.

"Not yet," Levi said. "This way."

We rounded the corner, walked by a narrow street that led to the back of the shopping center, flanked by snowbanks, and followed a little stone path into a bunch of leafless trees. After a few steps, the trees were gone and we entered what seemed like a small park. Despite the cold and the snow, people sat on benches feeding birds, walking their dogs or riding bikes along the concrete paths, and kids played on the playground. In an open area, a large pavilion stood with open sides, but for one wall with a big white screen. Lots of people sat on the picnic tables under the pavilion, and in the parking lot beside it were three food trucks.

"It's still the same," Levi mused, stopping at the edge of the stone path.

"What is?"

"Every Friday, they still have movie night here. But they used to put everything under tents. Now, they have that structure."

I frowned and glanced at the time on my phone. "There's still thirty minutes or so to dusk."

"People always came early to eat, let the kids play, talk with friends."

"It's so damn cold." Thankfully, Heidi's coat closet had plenty of Lacey's jackets and coats, and I grabbed a black one before Levi and I left the house.

"When you're born and raised in a cold town, you get used to it."

Kids ran from blanket to blanket. Some had frisbees and nerf guns, others played tag or hide-and-seek or were having a snowball fight. The adults gathered in groups and talked, laughed, and drank together.

It seemed like a perfect Friday evening for friends and family.

A pang of jealousy cut through my chest.

My family hadn't been that amazing, but I had had one.

Now, I had no idea what was going on with them, if they ever wondered what happened to me. Did they believe the rumors? Was it a rumor up there, or was it a fact? It really looked like it, the way the angels were hunting me.

I forced those thoughts out of my mind and turned my gaze to Levi, who watched the humans intently.

"How do you know Heidi?" I asked.

He turned cold eyes to me. "Will you drop it if I tell you to?"

I was curious, but I wouldn't bother him. "I will."

That half grin was back, but without its usual energy. "What did Lacey tell you, sweetheart?"

"Nothing."

"Liar. Lacey loves talking and she has no qualms talking about our past." He paused and looked out to the humans again, but I didn't think he was actually seeing them. "She doesn't have many friends in her coven. To be honest, she doesn't have any. She's seen as an outcast since she was born away from them and raised by a demon for the first nine years of her life."

"That's not her fault."

"Tell that to the coven." He shifted the paper bag to one hand and put the other inside the pocket of his slacks. "She longs for a friend, and to her, you seemed like a good candidate." He looked at me again. "Tell me, sweetheart, what did she tell you?"

"Nothing," I insisted. I didn't want to get Lacey in trouble.

Levi shook his head, and his hair fell over his eyes. "Heidi was hired as one of our nannies when we were kids," he finally answered my question. He pushed his hair back and returned his hand to his pocket. "She was the kindest, most caring nanny we had, and she actually stood up to our father whenever he threatened us." He inhaled deeply. "He got tired of it and fired her. We lost contact for many years."

"You haven't seen her in ... what? Ten years? This was the first time in ten-ish years?"

"Are you trying to do math, sweetheart? Or guess my age?" he asked, teasing me. He was correct on both accounts.

"Heidi left when I was sixteen and Lacey was eight." A year before Lacey was sent to live with her mother's coven. "But no, this wasn't the first we saw her in *twelve* years."

Which meant ... "You're twenty-eight. Or have you been twenty-eight for a while?" Lesser and neutral demons lived for a long time, but higher demons and princes were known to be immortal. Their aging slowed down around late teenage years, until it eventually stopped.

"I'm actually twenty-eight, Lacey is nineteen, and we'll probably stop aging in our mid-to-late thirties."

Hm, a new higher demon. You didn't meet one of those every day.

I went back to the previous subject. "How did you find Heidi again?"

He considered it, as if weighing the fact that he had already told me too much, and I shouldn't know more. I kind of agreed, but now I was curious.

"At thirteen, Lacey lost control of her magic when ..." He paused, shifted his weight. "When her period first came. I couldn't go to her, because the coven wouldn't allow it, and because I was tied up on business on the other side of the country. But I already had contacts. I was able to find Heidi in a matter of hours and begged her to go see Lacey."

"I bet you didn't need to beg."

He nodded. "I didn't. She was ready to go. Ever since then, we have maintained contact, the two of them more than me, but Heidi is like family. The good kind."

That was so sweet. Levi and Lacey had lost their mothers, but they had had a loving mother figure in their lives. I couldn't help but wonder why Heidi never had gotten married and had her own children ... that was a question for another day, though.

"I'm glad you have someone like her in your lives."

Levi turned fully to me, his eyes hard. "Lacey told you too much. Hell, me too, but it stops here, sweetheart. Do *not* let Lacey get close to you. She'll try, that's what she does, but you're going to push her away."

"Hey!" Who said I wanted to get close to her anyway?

"After all this shit is done, you'll cut this fucking bond, and you'll disappear from our lives. If you don't, I'll make you, and that will break her heart." He stepped closer, his powerful body casting a shadow over mine. "This is the only warning you'll get."

After a death glare, Levi walked away.

I waited a few steps and followed, since he was my ride back to Heidi's. If I had another way around, if I knew the town, I would have stayed here, probably watched the movie to clear my mind, and then found my own way back.

Maybe I still could. I didn't have the Uber app, but there were taxis. I just needed to find out Heidi's address.

"Come, sweetheart," Levi called out, his voice as harsh as before.

With a sigh, I trailed behind him.

Movement to my right caught my attention and I looked. I did a double take and came to a full stop.

"Levi," I said in a deep voice.

"What, sweetheart?" He continued walking for a few seconds, but when I didn't answer, he turned and followed my line of sight.

At the edge of the tree patch in the corner of the park, under the shadows cast by the trees, were two males in black hoodies.

"Demons," I said.

Levi nodded. "I can sense them."

I had lost most of that ability with my magic, but after so many years, I could tell. Besides, some of them didn't hide it.

Behind the duo, I could see more bobbing heads. It was a large group, and they were watching the families waiting for the movie.

"They will attack once its dark."

"It looks like it."

I looked at Levi, feeling a sense of urgency. "We have to stop them."

"What? We don't have to do anything."

"Levi, I can't just walk away from this."

"If we weren't here, if we hadn't come to meet Heidi, you wouldn't even know about this." Again, he approached me, towering over me. Was he trying to intimidate me with his impressive height? "Hell, with the demons banished from the underworld, there are thousands, tens of thousands of attacks like that happening right now all around the world. What are you going to do, sweetheart? Save them all?"

"I know I can't save them all, but I have to save the ones I can." I whirled on my heels, intent on rushing into the demons and fighting them in the trees.

How would I, a powerless creature, fight a handful of demons. But my principles wouldn't let me walk away from this.

A hand grabbed my wrist, pulling me back. Levi glared at me. "What the hell? Are you trying to get yourself killed?"

"Let me go." I jerked my arm hard, trying to get free, but his grip only intensified.

"I'm bound to you, sweetheart. If you go in there and die, because honestly, that's what will happen, and then what? I die too? Or the pain will be too much and it'll drive me crazy? I, for one, don't want to find out." He started walking away, holding tight to me, forcing me to come with him.

"Let me go, or I'll scream!"

He scoffed. "Do you think I care what the humans think, what they will do?"

I didn't. He could probably overpower a hundred humans, even armed ones, without breaking a sweat.

We exited the park the same way we came in. A few steps into the narrow road beside the shopping center, I jerked my arm again, trying to get free once more, and put all my weight behind it.

I stumbled back and Levi stopped, but his grip tightened.

"I'll scream!" I warned.

He leaned in. "Try it, sweetheart."

Shadows surged from the sides, and suddenly, we were surrounded.

My stomach dropped.

Shit, the demons had decided to come after us.

But when I looked around, I saw they were no demons.

They were Blackthorn Hunters and they had their Dawn-blades leveled at us.

I looked around for familiar faces and found a few.

"Erin? Rey?" I kept turning in a circle, taking them all in. "Doreen? Ava? Harvey?" I didn't know the other three hunters. "What's going on?"

For a moment, my heart squeezed. It was so good to see them. Rey was the headmaster of the Blackthorn Hunters Academy here in Colorado, and Erin, his girlfriend, was a princess of the underworld and one of the best demon hunters out there.

Ava and Harvey were their best friends and married to

each other, and Doreen was the hunter to call for any ridiculous mission. Or so I had heard.

Erin lowered her blade, her golden eyes inquisitive. "Ariella? What's going on?"

I glanced at Levi's grip on my wrist. "This ... it's nothing."

Rey took a step closer. The light of the setting sun cast a golden light over us, giving his brown hair a bronze shade. "It doesn't look like nothing."

Yeah, I could see why they would think that.

"He's a demon," Doreen said. She had beautiful auburn hair that I had always thought was too pretty to be real. "We should take him."

"You won't take me anywhere," Levi hissed.

"Stop," I told him in a lower voice, though I was sure everyone could hear me. "They are my friends."

"How comforting," Levi mused.

"What's going on? Why are you here?" I asked the hunters.

"We're tracking a group of lesser demons that has been terrorizing the nearby towns," Erin explained. She stared at Levi. "And we found a demon."

"No, no." I shook my head. "Levi has been with me for the past couple of days. Besides, we saw the group you're looking for." I pointed my free hand to the stone path. "Through there. They are hiding under the trees in the park."

Rey nodded to the hunters, and they jogged down the stone path. Erin stayed back.

"And what about this demon?" Rey asked.

"He's a higher demon," Erin said.

"Aren't you King Brikan's daughter?" Levi asked in that annoying, flirty tone. He did that on purpose, the bastard. "Princess of the Underworld."

"He's not king anymore, he's dead," Erin said. "And who are you?"

He took a step closer to her. "Wouldn't you like to know?"

Rey lifted his sword, blade at the ready.

"Ignore him," I said. "He's a pain in the ass, but he isn't evil. He's a good demon." The lie felt thick on my tongue, but I couldn't let them take him. "Besides, he's helping me."

"With what?" Rey asked.

I swallowed hard. It was no secret to our circle. "Find my wings." Though, I had never told anyone about my sword.

Erin's eyes widened. "What? You know where they are?"

I nodded. "Well, he does and he's taking me there."

Rey and Erin exchanged glances.

"Fine," Erin said. "We'll let you take him. But call us if things change." Erin handed me a black card. I slipped it into my pocket. A demon hunter with a business card—that was new. "Okay?"

"Of course."

"Actually, call me even if you don't need to," Erin said. "Text me your new number. Everyone has been trying to contact you for months."

I nodded. Once I lost my powers and left DuMoir Castle seven months ago, I received dozens of calls and hundreds of texts a day from my friends. I couldn't take it. I ended up changing my number so I would have some peace.

"I will," I lied. I would go straight to the underworld for the sheer amount of lies I had been telling lately.

"I mean it," Erin said. "Everyone is worried about you, especially Farrah and Wyatt. After you get your wings back, you should give them a call."

I nodded, not willing to say anything else.

Rey stared at Levi, looking as menacing as the demon. "If you hurt her, we'll find you, and we'll make you regret it."

I didn't waste my breath saying Levi couldn't hurt me. That information wasn't important.

"Thank you," I said.

"We should go," Rey said.

"We should." Erin reached out, squeezed my hand, and then followed to catch up to the other hunters.

I stared at the path long after they disappeared.

"You're such a liar, sweetheart."

I snapped my head back to Levi. "What?"

"You won't call anyone."

No, I wouldn't, but I wouldn't give him the satisfaction of agreeing with him. I jerked my hand again. "They will capture those demons. You can let me go now."

Levi hesitated but withdrew his hand.

His grip had left a red mark around my wrist and I rubbed at it. Jerk. Didn't it hurt him too? Or was this kind of pain a tickle for him?

For a moment, I considered going after Erin and Rey and the others and helping them. That was what I used to do ... when I had my powers.

I had to be real with myself. I wouldn't be able to help a fly now if it yelled for me. I would only put myself in danger and my friends would have to rescue me.

I walked past Levi, toward the car. "Let's get out of here."

12

———

Levi and I didn't talk on the way back to Heidi's house. In the driveway, he grabbed our bags from the car's trunk and marched into the house, leaving me behind.

Not that I was in any mood to spend more time with him.

But inside the house, I couldn't avoid him for long. I went to the kitchen, and found him at the bay window, spying on the shed.

"They're still at it." He walked to the fridge, put the lasagna in, and typed something on his phone. "I sent a text to Lacey about the food."

I glanced at the shed, the doors wide open and light streaming from it, and more shame coursed through me. They were working nonstop to make my potion, to help me, a stranger who had suddenly busted into their lives.

"Holy hell, I can feel that," Levi snapped. "Your ... what? Embarrassment? Your guilt? Why? It wasn't your fault you lost your wings and your magic, was it? Unless you're hiding something."

"It's not just that." My cheeks flamed. "I'm not used to

people helping me for nothing." It was usually the opposite. "I hate standing on the side, waiting. I want to help."

"Oh, the little fallen angel can't sit pretty?" He showed me that incorrigible lopsided grin. "At least you got the pretty part down, sweetheart."

My brows curled down. This was the second time he'd implied I was pretty. Why was he doing that?

"Stop calling me sweetheart."

The mischief in his eyes told me he never would. "Stop calling me Levi."

"Not a chance."

"There you have it," he said. "I'm out for the night. I'll put your bag in your bedroom." He walked out of the kitchen, and I almost marched after him.

Why was he so annoying? Why did I get so annoyed with him? I could ignore him.

With that gorgeous face, that deep voice, that brilliant stare, dazzling smile, and powerful presence, I doubted anyone could ignore him.

By the light, there went my thoughts again.

I berated myself and marched up the stairs to a long corridor with several doors. Only two were open: a bathroom and a guest bedroom with two single beds. My bag was on one of the beds.

It was early to turn in for the night, but I was tired, and despite being healed from the poison, my almost-human body could use the rest.

I grabbed a long, black shirt I used as a nightdress and clean undies, and tiptoed to the bathroom in the hallway, hoping not to bump into Levi.

Or hoping *to*.

What the hell?

I showered, washed my hair—thank goodness there was everything one could need in the shower and under the sink—and went back to the bedroom. I closed the door behind me, turned off the lights, and slipped under the covers.

My body was tired, by my mind was reeling.

I wished there was a button that I could press to turn it all off for a few hours. That would be bliss.

As it was, I twisted and turned for what felt like hours.

IN THE DEMON'S CLAWS, RACHEL LOOKED AT ME, HER EYES FULL OF despair. "Run."

Molraz dropped her body and zeroed in on me, on the object in my hands.

Panic flooded my veins and I ran.

I sat up in bed, breathing hard, my heart thumping against my rib cage like a hammer.

It took me a second to remember where I was, that I was safe. The bedroom was dark, with only a sliver of light coming from under the half-closed curtains, and Lacey slept on the bed beside mine.

I hadn't even seen her come in.

I placed a hand over my frantic heart and took a deep breath, forcing myself to calm down.

It had been a nightmare. I hadn't had one of those in so long ...

I had to remember, they couldn't touch me. Not here, not now, not with this ward or the necklace. Soon, I would have my wings back, and hopefully information from the higher demon who had ripped them off. He would tell me what the hell had happened that night, what had gone wrong, and then I would kill him.

I lay back in bed, closed my eyes, and tried to go back to sleep.

But all I saw was the nightmare, all I felt was the terror of that night.

Knowing I couldn't sleep anymore, I grabbed my phone—it was just past two in the morning!—and tiptoed downstairs. In the kitchen, I filled a glass with chilled water and drank half of it in one go.

Not sure what to do with myself, I walked outside. From the porch, I could see the shed, this time closed, and though there was no one there now, I knew the potion was in there, brewing away.

Barefoot, I padded to the grass, felt the cool blades on my toes and inhaled the fresh, chill night air. I let it fill my lungs, clear my mind, propel my blood, give me renewed energy.

This was paradise. I knew it was probably twenty-five degrees if I went to the front of the house, but here it was a perfect seventy-five. Heidi was probably powerful enough to keep this spell up all the time.

Without thinking, I lay on the cool grass, the blades tickling my bare legs, and stared at the night sky. A few clouds hovered in my peripheral vision, and I couldn't see the moon, but mostly, the sky was dotted with millions of bright stars.

Humans believed that heaven was somewhere among the stars. That was a beautiful way of thinking about my home, but like the underworld, Elysium could only be reached by portals. Angels with wings could cross the portals freely, but others, including angels without wings, had to ask permission. If they tried to go through without permission, the portal would block them.

I know, because I had tried.

More than once.

More than a hundred times.

That was how desperate I was after I was abandoned here.

Why were my thoughts veering toward terrible things again?

I closed my eyes and inhaled deeply, welcoming the scent of the grass, the perfume of the trees behind the shed, and even a handful of spices from the shed.

Then another scent invaded my nostrils.

A deep wood and musk scent, along with something masculine.

I opened my eyes as Levi stepped up closer and bent his torso over me, obscuring my view of the sky.

"A night escapade, sweetheart? Didn't peg you as that kind."

I scoffed. "And what did you peg me as?"

He sidestepped me and sat on the grass beside me. "A fierce and righteous angel."

That was a nice compliment.

He looked nice too. He wore black silk pants and a white t-shirt that hugged his sinful body in the most appealing way. Were these his pajamas? Jeez, even that was attractive on him.

Then I realized something and sat up. "Shit, I woke you up."

"Yes. I felt your terror. Nightmare?"

I nodded. "Something like that."

"Want to talk about it?"

I raised my eyebrows at him. "What happened to the I-don't-do-small-talk speech?"

He lay on the grass and folded his arms behind his head,

his biceps bulging with the movement. "If talking helps you relax and go back to sleep, so I can sleep too, I'm all ears, sweetheart."

I stared at him while he stared at the night sky. Could Heidi be right? Did he have a good heart? Even half of one? But he was a higher demon.

I couldn't say I knew a full-blooded demon, other than the ones I had fought against with my friends, and those had definitely been evil. But I'd met half demons before, like Erin and Rey, and they were good people, with good hearts, and only acted for the greater good of everyone, supernaturals and humans alike.

I hadn't been there, but I had heard about the meeting where Erin had called every leader she knew or had heard of in the supernatural world, and she told them that not all half demons were bad, not all vampires were blood-sucking cannibals, not all wolves were hot-tempered to the point of murder, and so on. Like humans, all supernaturals came in every shade of gray possible.

Perhaps even full-blooded demons.

But for some reason, Levi hid it all underneath a thick layer of mean, and I was suddenly dying to know why.

I lay back beside him. "There's nothing to tell."

"Then what can I do for you to go back to sleep?"

"Sing me a lullaby," I teased.

"Sweetheart, I do have a good voice, but you're not about to hear it."

We stared at the stars for a moment, in comfortable silence, the only sound around us were the crickets and insects in the grass and the woods.

What was happening here? A couple of days ago, I wouldn't have thought I could relax beside Levi, much less feel this nagging pull to tell him the truth about my situation.

Why *shouldn't* I tell him? What would he do? He wouldn't call the angels and deliver me on a silver platter, not while the bond held and he couldn't hurt me.

If I told him, maybe, just maybe, the sliver of good in his heart would sympathize with me, with my cause, and he would be more willing to help me, bond or not.

I turned my head and looked at him.

Damn, he was fine; it was almost painful. Why would a demon look this good? I knew why. Like vampires, some of them used beauty to draw their victims in.

And I was falling for it right now.

"You're staring, sweetheart."

"I'm wondering if I should tell you about my nightmare," I said, only half of it. I would never admit he was handsome.

Levi twisted, turning sideways to me, placed his elbow on the grass and his fist on his temple. "Tell me, sweetheart. Anything to empty that pretty head and let me sleep."

Pretty?

It was probably like when he called me sweetheart. Just another piece of his game. It meant nothing.

I looked up at the stars again, not sure I could face him while I told him my story.

"Soon after I graduated from Guardian Academy, I volunteered for a mission on Earth with some of the best archangels and Seraphim in Elysium. One of my mentors, an archangel, said it was a big mission and I wasn't ready, but another archangel thought I was. He said it was time for me to join the ranks of famous guardians." The moment had made me feel proud. "So, we got a team of twelve. Two archangels, four Seraphim, and six Cherubin—me included."

Among the other five Cherubin were my best friend Rachel and my crush Jeremiah. They had graduated with me and had been invited on this mission. That had been the main reason I had requested to go. How could they get all the glory while I waited my turn?

"What was your mission?"

"To come to Earth to find a rogue angel who was feeding valuable information to a higher demon. We searched for two days until we finally found him ... or so we thought. It was a trap. The higher demon, Molraz, was there waiting for us with dozens of his demons."

"You mentioned the demon before."

I nodded. "Yeah. I think he orchestrated everything with Rhodes."

"The archangel?"

"Yes. He turned on us and killed Soren." My throat closed. I didn't think I had ever talked about this mission to anyone, not even to Farrah and Wyatt, a fae and a wolf shifter, who became my first real friends here on Earth. "Two other Seraphim joined Rhodes and attacked us. We weren't prepared for that betrayal. It was a bloodbath."

I swallowed hard.

I still remembered how Rachel collapsed on me, half dead. The same agony, the same despair from that day clawed its way up my chest as the screams, the scent of blood filled my senses.

"Hey." Levi touched my shoulder, his fingers featherlight. "Look at me." I blinked and turned my head to him, looking into his eyes. "It's over. They can't get you now. Okay?"

I nodded, but a sob caught in my throat. "They are after me right now."

He frowned. "The demons?"

"No, the angels." I shook my head. "I was one of the last ones still alive, still fighting. Molraz came for me, and I tried to flee. He destroyed my Celestial Sword and ripped my wings off." The pain had been so great, I thought I was going to die right then. "He joked he would keep them as a memento from the best Cherubin he had fought against in centuries."

"That's why you want to find him. You think he really has your wings."

I shrugged. "You tell me." His body stiffened. "You're the one who saw my wings. Was it his house you saw?"

Levi averted his eyes. "I don't know whose house it was."

"I know you don't. Anyway, after he got my wings, he tried to kill me, but I fled." I didn't want to give him all bloody details of that horrible experience. And what I had with me when I ran. "Like a coward."

"How did you escape them, sweetheart?"

"I ran as fast as I could until I found a cliff with a river below. I jumped."

He frowned. "And they let you go?"

I shook my head. "No, they came after me, but ... I don't know. Luck was on my side?" Once I would have said Adona had been watching over me, but these were her warriors, following her orders. I didn't know anything anymore. "I ended up farther down the river, and I didn't stop moving for days. At some point, they lost my trail."

I had been half dead, and if I hadn't bumped into a witch who nursed me back to health and minimized the scars from my wings, I would probably have died.

"You were certainly very lucky."

"I know." But to what end? To live the rest of my life on the run? "After I healed, I tried contacting my mentor. I wanted to tell her Rhodes had betrayed us all, but turns out, Rhodes told them I was the traitor. I don't know the details; I can't contact anyone in Elysium. I heard this from people who have heard from others, but apparently, Rhodes said I had made an alliance with Molraz and attacked them. I was the reason only he had survived, but he saw that as a sign to hunt me down and make me pay for my crimes."

"That's why you're running."

I nodded. "I need to find Molraz and make him confess about his alliance with Rhodes. Then with my wings, I can enter Elysium."

Rhodes would be arrested and punished, and I would be welcomed back home.

"What do you think Rhodes wanted to do? Kill a bunch of angels? That was it?"

My face grew hot. "Molraz probably knows Rhodes's plan, or at least a piece of it." I had no idea what his plan was, if he had already succeeded, if he had killed the angels. I believed he needed the item I had stolen, and thus hadn't achieved his goal yet, but it had been so long. At some point, he would find an alternative.

That was another reason I needed to go back. I had to know.

"How long ago was that?"

"Five-ish years."

Levi scoffed. "Who said Rhodes hasn't succeeded already?"

I knew he hadn't, and I was the reason for that. But that part was better forgotten. "He hasn't, or the entire supernatural world would have heard about it."

"I guess you're right." He fixed his eyes on mine. "So here I am, a higher demon helping a Cherubin uncover a dirty plan and take down the traitor to save heaven. That will not be good for my reputation, sweetheart."

A small smile spread over my lips. "I bet you can tarnish your reputation again. Do something big, and everyone will forget you played the hero for a few days."

He leaned a little closer and lowered his voice. "Are you telling me to be bad, sweetheart?" His gaze flicked to my lips and warmth spread over my stomach.

"Maybe," I whispered.

Levi inched closer as he licked his lips, his eyes back on mine. I arched my back, erasing the distance between us.

A broken twig echoed through the backyard, and Levi and I jumped to our feet.

A small fox spied from behind a bush before leaping back into the woods.

I placed a hand over my racing heart and inhaled deeply.

"I almost incinerated the little guy," Levi said, putting out the darkfire that enveloped his arms.

"I know, I thought it was the angels," I said.

I turned to him, but he was already looking at me. His eyes traveled down my body, lingering on my naked legs.

Levi took a full step back then turned his half grin on. "Did the therapy session work, sweetheart? If it did, you should go back to bed."

My brow furrowed. "What about you?

His blue eyes flamed. "After that, I think I need a beer."

After what? The almost kiss or the fox?

Did it matter?

I nodded, turning to the porch. Stopped. "Good night, Levi."

The grin was still plastered across his lips, but it didn't have the same glow as before. "Night, sweetheart."

Half of me was relieved the kiss didn't happen, and the other half was disappointed. What would it be like to kiss Levi? He was so intense, so dark, so menacing, I bet his kisses would be the same.

Pushing those thoughts out of my head, I walked inside the house and headed to bed.

I turned in bed, hugged the pillow, and tried going back to my dream. I didn't remember the details, but this time, it had been a nice one. I didn't want to wake up and face the reality of my life, which was definitely not that nice.

But I couldn't force myself to fall asleep again. With a groan, I reached for my phone on the nightstand and turned on the screen.

"What?" I sat up, startled it was already nine thirty in the morning.

I was on a freaking mission, not on vacation. I got up, used the restroom, washed my face with soap, brushed my teeth, and got dressed in black faux-leather leggings, a white tank top, and my combat boots.

I found Lacey in the kitchen, with her hair tied in a ponytail and wearing a teal apron. She looked from the range to me and smiled. "Good morning!"

"Morning." I walked up to the middle of the kitchen and saw she had breakfast well underway and the table was set for four. "Why didn't you wake me up?"

She shrugged and flipped a pancake in the frying pan. "You were sleeping so peacefully, and I knew the potion wouldn't be ready yet, so why not? Did you sleep well?"

"Ye—"

I heard a murmur and glanced out the bay window. Levi paced on the porch, his phone pressed against his ear.

Had he been up for long? Was he already working? Getting some innocent tangled up in his wishes? It was better if I imagined him to be an evil demon, this way I could protect myself.

Protect my heart.

"Ariella?"

I snapped my head back at Lacey, who had a smile on her lips. Shit.

"Hm, yes, I slept great. How about you?"

"Me too." She put two pancakes in a pile. "Can you get the others, please? Breakfast will be ready in two minutes."

I glanced around. "Where's Heidi?"

"In the shed," Lacey said.

I looked at the shed through the window. The door was wide open and I could see movement on the inside, even though I couldn't distinguish what was happening exactly.

I started for the door, but it opened and Levi stepped in. "Don't worry, sweetheart, I've got Heidi."

"Morning to you too," I muttered.

He walked past me and got some of the plates from Lacey. "Good news. I talked to Burgin, one of my men. He found out who the mansion belongs to." He brought the plates to the table. "It's not Molraz."

My stomach dropped. "It's not?"

"No." He slipped on to the bench and started piling his plate with pancakes, scrambled eggs, and bacon. "It's another demon who supposedly buys extremely rare supernatural items on the black market. His human name is Duncan Kensington and his house has a state-of-the-art security system, plus a dozen guards and dogs trained to attack."

"Paranoid much?" Lacey turned off the stove and joined us at the table.

Levi shrugged. "I would be too if the contents of my mansion were estimated at over seven billion dollars."

"Wait." I raised a finger. "Are you saying my wings have a price tag?"

"From what I heard, he bought them on the black market, sweetheart."

My stomach turned and I almost snapped at him, but I knew it wasn't his fault. I was the one who had lost them and now I was paying for it.

"What's the plan? We'll raid his house?"

"Actually, Burgin already contacted his guy. He won't meet with us, but his secretary, Lars, will."

"What do you mean? How did you do that?"

"I told him I have a rare item his boss will want to acquire, and I would love to discuss the details." He winked at me. "I'm full of tricks, sweetheart."

"Oh, I know."

My cheeks flamed after I said that. He had probably been tricking me last night when he almost kissed me, and I would have fallen for it.

Lacey glanced from him to me, and back at him.

"Anyway, sweetheart, we leave as soon as we eat and get the potion from Heidi."

"It should be ready soon," Lacey said. "Then you two can go."

"You two? You're not going?"

She shook her head, her expression dejected. "I'll stay with Heidi for a few days. She needs my help."

I opened my mouth to protest. She was stepping away to let her brother throw his charms at me, and I would fall, I knew I would. I wasn't as strong as I wanted to be. It might be a great one-night stand, but damn, I didn't have time for that.

Before I could say anything, the door opened and Heidi entered the kitchen. She dragged her feet to the table and stared at us with a smile.

"It's so good to see my house so lively," she said, her voice frail.

My heart gave a little squeeze. The old witch looked a lot older today. Her hair needed a good brush, her clothes were rumpled, and there were heavy bags under her eyes. Even her movements were slower than before, as if it was hard to move.

I glanced at Lacey and her eyes told me everything. That was why she was staying, because from last evening to now something had drained Heidi's energy ... and that something was me. Or rather, the potion she had made for me.

The hand around my heart clutched harder.

Still smiling, Heidi slipped onto the seat beside Lacey and handed me what looked like a glorified shoebox. "The potions."

I opened the lid and gawked at it. There were so many ... I did a quick estimate, and if I was right, there was enough to last me two months. "This is amazing." I closed the lid. "But this is too much. These potions cost a lot, I know that. It can't be a gift and—"

"Pfft, that's nonsense." Heidi waved a hand at me. "It wasn't expensive at all." Her gaze flicked to Levi, who continued eating as if nothing was happening.

What was that?

"I insist."

"It's a gift to my favorite angel," she said.

A small smile tugged at my lips. "I'm probably the only angel you know."

She winked at me. "Exactly."

"Seriously, though, I can't—"

The smile was gone. "Ariella, I'm an old and powerful witch and I'm telling you this is a gift. Now take them and be happy before I turn you into a toad!"

For a second, the entire table was quiet and tense.

Then Lacey let out a howler of a laugh, Heidi's laughter sounded more like hiccups, and even Levi's shoulder shook as he tried to hide he was laughing.

I smiled at her. "Thank you. Really. You might not want money, but I'll repay you for your kindness someday."

She finally cut a piece of her pancake, put it in her mouth, and said before she started chewing, "That I wouldn't mind."

WHEN LEVI DROVE AWAY FROM DURANGO, HIS HANDS ON THE wheel, and me in the passenger seat beside him, I finally asked him.

"What did you do?"

"You have to be more specific, sweetheart, because I do a lot of things." His tone was flirty, casual, but I was sure he knew what I was talking about.

"You paid for the potions."

"Nah—" He glanced at me and probably saw the teasing was over. At least for now. "Whatever you're thinking, that's not it, sweetheart. I'm doing this for selfish reasons. If you get caught, you'll get hurt, and if you get hurt, I'll get hurt."

"How much was it?"

"It doesn't matter. Like Heidi said, it's a gift."

"It matters to me." I wanted to take note of it so one day I could repay him. I really didn't want to owe money to a demon. Even if he said it was a gift now, he could use that against me in the future. I would repay him with money and Heidi with kindness or help. She had done a lot for me. "All right, don't tell me. I can use the price I paid for them in Houston and make my own calculations."

"Sweetheart, just—"

I glared at him and he shut up.

Another ten minutes of tense silence went by before I worked up the courage to ask. "What happened to Heidi? She seemed well yesterday, and today, it was like she had only twenty percent of her energy left." It couldn't be the potions, could it?

"Heidi is a lot older than you think, and she has been dealing with arthritis. Every time she uses her magic, it flares up."

"What? But that's a human disease."

"Tell that to her body. Lacey is a great healer and she can't get rid of it. She can make Heidi feel better, though."

"That's why she stayed."

Levi nodded, his eyes on the road. "With the proper rest and Lacey's magic, Heidi will be like new in no time."

I could see he really cared for Heidi, like he cared for Lacey. And the women cared for him too.

I reached up and touched the necklace around my neck. When I tried giving it back, Heidi told me to keep it. "It belonged to a good friend. It has been sitting in a drawer for far too long. I would be glad if you kept it."

That had melted my heart. How could I say no to that?

I pushed those thoughts away before they even started and reached for something else. "Hm, are my clothes good enough for a meeting with the secretary of a billionaire demon?"

That half grin was back. "I have a plan for that."

14

I couldn't believe we were in Las Vegas.

Even with short notice, Levi was able to book a fancy suite in one of the best hotels in the city. I stood in front of the floor-to-ceiling window of the common seating room that divided our bedrooms, and stared at the famous Vegas Strip. I had been here before. Hell, was there a place I didn't know in the United States and Canada? But I hadn't stayed long, and I certainly hadn't enjoyed the nightlife here.

As an angel on the run, all I could do was hide.

"Ready, sweetheart?"

I turned around and sucked in a sharp breath.

Levi stood about five feet from me, wearing a black suit with a teal button-up shirt, the top three buttons undone. The color of the shirt made his blue eyes pop, and the suit hugged his impressive shoulders exactly right. He had combed his bangs back, and probably put on gel to make them stay, and he had such an elegant air.

Damn, he looked fine.

More than fine. He looked totally hot.

His eyes ran the length of me twice before fixing on mine.

"You're stunning," he said, not one hint of teasing in his deep voice.

Heat spread over my cheeks.

Before we made it to the hotel, we had stopped by a store to buy our clothes for the meeting. Turned out, the meeting was in a nightclub for supernaturals and we had to dress up. I had gone to the women's section, while Levi had gone to the men's, and we hadn't seen each other's purchase until now—though he had paid for mine.

I chose a black mini dress with lace for the top, with only a thin band of black fabric to cover my breasts, and a deep V down the back. The dress was skintight and required me to wear one of those backless bras—thankfully, they had those at the store too. They also had makeup, which I never carried with me, so after taking a shower and washing and drying my hair, I applied a little dark shadow around my eyes and a cherry lipstick.

To complete the look, I had bought dangling silver earrings and black stilettos.

I did feel stunning, but I was sure he had seen plenty of gorgeous women in his life, probably dressed much better and sexier than me. He was being a charmer again, and it bothered me a little.

"Thank you," I finally said. "You don't look so bad yourself."

The lopsided grin stamped his perfect lips. "We both know I look handsome, sweetheart."

Damn right.

He offered me the thin jacket I had bought to go with the dress—Las Vegas was chilly at night in February—then he offered me his arm. I hesitated but took both. We left the hotel and walked the short blocks to our destination, Temptation. From the outside, it looked like a normal nightclub among the casinos and shops, but Levi had told me about it.

He had even tried to persuade me to sit this one out.

"There are only supernaturals in there," he had told me. "And not good ones. The club ... it's not a normal nightclub. It's dark, it's almost forbidden, which attracts lots of shady figures. And an angel won't be allowed in, unless ..." And then he told me his plan.

I didn't like it one bit, but if it was the only way for me to go to this meeting with him, then so be it. This entire thing was about my wings, finding Molraz and exacting my revenge. Levi wasn't about to do this alone.

At the entrance, Levi showed the bouncer the invitation on his phone. The bouncer stepped aside and opened the door for us.

We stepped into what seemed to be a dark room, but my sight quickly adjusted to the black light. At the end of the narrow room stood two other bouncers and silver double doors. As we walked toward the doors, one of the bouncers asked if I wanted to leave my jacket in their coatroom. I did. Then they opened them and music, colorful lights, and the heavy scent of alcohol and perfume spilled out.

Levi put his hand over mine on his arm as we walked past them, into the nightclub. The doors were closed behind us and the *thump thump* of the loud electronic music shook the floors, the walls, and my skull.

I took the place in, unimpressed. It was a long, rectangular room, with a sunken level in the middle, where the dance floor was. Red, green, blue, and pink lights coming from the tall ceiling swirled around the dancers. Tables and booths surrounded the dance floor, all of them taken, and on the back was a long bar, also full of customers. The place wasn't packed, but it was full enough.

I leaned closer to Levi and almost yelled, "This is it?"

"This is the first room, sweetheart," he said. "It's the tame one."

I frowned. "You have been here before."

He dipped his chin. "Once, and it wasn't by choice." He slipped my hand from the crook of his elbow to his hand and entwined his fingers with mine. "Ready?"

No, I wasn't. But did I have any choice?

I nodded.

We weaved through the crowd. I couldn't help glance at them as we went. I could tell right away what some of them were. The vampires had their fangs out, the fae didn't hide their ears, some witches carried wands or potions, and I even saw a wolf shifter with his ears and claws shifted.

Some of them glanced our way, and like Levi had said, most did a double take and stared at me, disdain clear on their faces.

Yup, they didn't like angels.

And it upset me that they could sense that, even though I didn't have my wings or my magic.

When a shifter, I couldn't tell which kind, snarled at us, Levi pulled me to him. "Stay close, sweetheart," he said in my ear.

Then, when I thought he was taking me to a dark corner, we turned to the left beside the bar and entered another small room, like the lobby—dark lights, two supernaturals and double doors.

Levi flashed the invitation again and the bouncers opened the doors. These led to wide, black-carpeted stairs. Once more, the doors were closed once we walked through them, but this time, it felt different.

The music here was calmer, lower, and the walls didn't shake. The stairs curved down for what felt like two stories, until they opened into a landing.

Levi paused there, close to the silver railing. "And here it is."

Still holding his hand, I stood with him and glanced down. With the dark lights and the few colored spotlights, it was hard to note every detail, but even then, I could see the place was at least three times the size of upstairs, at least four times as tall, and divided into several sections. The dance floor was once again right in the middle and this time, the supernaturals danced to pop music as if they were having sex right there. The bar was right beside the dance floor and cut from one end of the room to the other, through the different zones. Servers carried glasses filled with neon drinks up and down, and I even saw—

"Is that blood?" I did my best not to point.

"Oh, it is." Levi gestured to another zone, where low couches and booths created a maze.

I saw a couple seated in a corner of the booth leaning into each other, lying down on the black leather. Then the male reached up and closed a black curtain around them. That was when I noticed the black portions I had assumed were walls were actually curtains.

"You can close yourself off," I muttered. "And ...?"

Levi showed me that grin of his. "Do whatever you want, sweetheart. Have sex, do drugs ... And vampires go there to drink blood directly from the source. At least, the ones who don't want others to see."

A little disturbed, I glanced to another section: a place

with lots of tables and armchairs, and several podiums among them—with almost naked dancers. Some podiums had only one dancer, but two of them had two dancers, and the largest one had three. They moved sensually, touching each other, licking, rubbing their pelvis, making faces that should be reserved for bed.

It was almost vulgar and I should be appalled. I was, a little, but still, I couldn't help but feel a little turned on by the sight.

Levi cleared his throat. His hand squeezed mine. "Let's go."

We descended the rest of the stairs and found ourselves in an open area under the ledge. From there, we could choose which direction to go, which zone to explore.

Without wasting time, Levi veered us to the table zone. As soon as we started walking through the tables, supernaturals started looking at us—at me. Levi let go of my hand, but put his entire arm behind me, his hand splayed on the small of my back, his fingertips over the curve of my ass. I wanted to elbow him and tell him to go to hell, but I knew I had to stay in character.

One shifter snarled at me, and Levi's fingertips dug into my skin, but he pretended to not see it. Two vampires rose from their seats and sniffed the air.

"Her blood smells sweet," one said.

"Pure," said the other.

Levi glared at them but didn't say anything.

I turned my face to Levi, batting my lashes at him. His plan was that the supernaturals would leave me alone in the club if I pretended to be his. A demon who had broken an angel and claimed her for himself. I had to pretend to be infatuated with him, otherwise, I would either be kicked out, captured, or killed.

None of those options sounded attractive to me.

We approached a long table at the end of the zone, with several armchairs and three of them occupied by males. I could tell one was a shifter, the other a half demon, but I had no idea what the third was.

"That's Lars," Levi told me jerking his chin toward the unknown supernatural. The collector's secretary.

"What is he?"

"Half warlock, and ..." He paused, inhaled deeply. "I don't know what else."

Suddenly, a huge man stepped in our way. A bear shifter.

"We have an appointment with Lars," Levi said, flashing his charming smile.

"He's busy right now," the bear shifter said. "You can wait, though this could take hours."

Levi tensed beside me, but his face didn't show anything. "And where can I wait?"

"Anywhere," the bear said. "We'll call you when he is ready for you."

I could feel that didn't sit well with Levi. It didn't sit well with me either. If I didn't know I would be flagged, I would have yelled at this shifter and made Lars see us now.

Instead, I draped myself on Levi. "Buy me a drink," I said, not recognizing the sugary tone coming out of my mouth.

Levi turned his lopsided smile to me. "Of course, sweetheart."

With his possessive hand on my back, Levi steered us toward the bar at the edge of the dance floor. He sat on the only free stool and pulled me on top of him.

Oh, damn.

My body coiled, I sat sideways over his thick thighs, careful to cross my legs because of my short dress. Levi's hand continued on my back, and the other he called on a bartender and ordered a whiskey for himself and a red wine for me.

Then he leaned into me, whispering in my ear, "Relax, sweetheart. Everyone is watching."

It was hard to relax like this. I turned my face to him and found his mouth only an inch from mine. Looking into his eyes, I slid one of my arms under his suit jacket and scratched my nails on his back.

His eyes darkened.

I brushed my lips on his ear. "Better?"

He let out something that sounded like a growl. "Careful, sweetheart, or I'll think you're really into it."

Was there any way I couldn't be? This place reeked of sex, the people were well dressed and sexy, the dancers turned everyone on, and the man under me was sin incarnate.

I dragged my lips down his throat and Levi's free hand closed on the side of my waist, tight.

When the drinks came, I drank a sip of my wine and Levi downed his whiskey in one swallow. Holding me, he stood and helped me to my feet.

"We're going to dance." He grabbed my hand and pulled me to the dance floor.

I almost dropped the wineglass as I put it back on the bar and went with him. He weaved to the center of the dance floor, where a mass of bodies ground against each other, and I was sure a guy had his hand under a girl's skirt.

The song was a slow pop ballad, with sexy beats, and when Levi knotted his arm around my waist, I couldn't help but dance. I moved my hips and Levi moved with me, matching my rhythm.

I grabbed his arms, his hard biceps under my hands, and he clutched my waist, keeping me close.

He stared at me for a moment, his eyes dark and full of lust.

There was no denying, I felt it too. Intoxicated by the music, the scene, and the company, I slid my hands around Levi's shoulders and glued my chest to his. Now, when we moved, every inch of our bodies rubbed against the other, creating delicious friction.

Levi's hand found my hair and he tugged back, exposing my neck. He grazed his lips up my throat and heat spread low in my belly. I had to bite down on my lip to suppress a moan.

His breath was heavy in my ear. "What are you trying to do, sweetheart?"

"I'm just playing my role," I said seriously. But inside, every cell of my body was coiling, the friction too good to ignore.

He slid a hand down my ass and pressed it hard against him. My breath caught when I felt the bulge against my lower stomach. "That's how well you're playing."

Holy shit, I was losing my mind, because for a moment, I even considered taking Levi back to the curtains area, so I could have my way with him.

Damn, I hadn't had sex in so long, I wasn't sure I even knew how it worked anymore. But suddenly, I wanted to find out.

I turned around, pressing my back to his front and swaying my hips sensually with the beat of the music across his crotch, his hard-on too big to miss. One of Levi's hands splayed low on my belly, pushing me hard against him, the other landed below my breast.

I threw my head back, resting it on his shoulder.

Levi lowered his head to my neck and snarled, "Ariella."

"What?" I asked, breathless, provoking.

"You—" Suddenly Levi stiffened, his hand still possessive, and he glanced to the side.

"He'll see you now," the bear shifter said. His eyes stayed on me for a second too long and Levi snarled.

The shifter huffed and walked away.

Without looking at me, Levi dropped his hands and took a long step back.

A coldness washed over me. The lust was still very much alive, but I felt a level of self-consciousness now that brought on mortification.

By the light, what had I done?

I was seconds from pushing Levi to a corner and begging him to take me. In the middle of a nightclub. With lots of people around us. No, not people. Evil supernaturals.

What the hell was wrong with me?

Levi finally looked at me and offered me his hand, his trademark grin on his face. "Ready, sweetheart?"

Was it me, or did this grin lack the intensity of the previous one? Wasn't his tone cheerful?

No, I was probably imagining things.

Still having a role to play, I slipped my hand in his and let him guide me back to the tables.

This time, Lars was seated at the head of the long table by himself. When we approached, the bear shifted showed us to two armchairs on his right side.

As we sat down, Levi shook Lars's hand. "Leviathan."

"I've heard of you before, Leviathan."

"Bad things, I hope."

Lars chuckled. "You can say that." He glanced at me but seeing me as Levi's pet, he ignored me. "So, I heard you have something of interest."

"Yes, I have a collector's piece, actually, and I would love to show your boss."

"My boss?"

"Duncan Kensington."

"Ah, I see." He sounded irritated now. "Duncan is my business partner, not my boss." Oh, shit, this wasn't going well. "And my part of the business is to see all pieces and make selections."

"That's a big part of the business," Levi said, as if he had already forgotten calling Duncan his boss. "I don't have the piece with me, but I can show you a picture." Levi grabbed his phone from the pocket inside his jacket.

"It's not necessary," Lars said.

"So, you'll arrange a meeting?"

Lars stared at Levi for a moment before shaking his head. "No. Whatever you have, I'm certain neither I nor Duncan are interested in it." His eyes shifted to me. "Unless you have an angel for sale."

My stomach tightened and Levi stiffened. He rose to his feet. "I think we're done here."

I held on to Levi's hand and tugged him down. We couldn't go. This couldn't end like this. We had to secure a meeting with Duncan, preferably at his house, where my wings were being kept.

"Levi," I whispered.

He slid his other hand under my elbow and pulled me up with him. "In case you change your mind about the item"—he dropped a black card on the table—"here's my number."

With that, Levi turned and walked away, towing me with him.

"But—"

"Shh." His eyes darted side-to-side. "Not here."

I glanced around and saw what he meant. Now, every supernatural around the tables was looking at us. "Hurry," he whispered.

We were halfway through the stairs, on the landing, when three males ran up toward us.

"Where do you think you're going?"

15

I COULDN'T HELP BUT GLANCE AT THEM.

"Aren't you that angel?" one of them asked.

My steps faltered, but Levi kept going, dragging me with him.

"Yeah, the one who killed her entire team," a second one said. "I'm sure it's her."

I turned to them now, appalled. Where had they heard that? I thought only the angels knew about it.

"It is you, isn't it?" the third one asked, closing in.

Levi jerked me forward but stopped three steps later as two other supernaturals stood in the way.

"Gentleman," he started, turning in a circle. "You're mistaken. This angel here has been my pet for many years now and—"

"Stop the bullshit," a vampire said as he joined the group. Another handful of supernaturals came up the stairs. "Hand that angel over."

Now, more guests looked up from the nightclub, wondering what was happening or recognizing me. Which didn't make sense. How did they know about that day? How did they know what I looked like?

"When I say, we run," Levi whispered, so low, I hoped no vampire or wolf shifter or fae had heard it. I gave him a slight nod. "Sure," Levi said, nonchalant. "Just take my angel." He threw his hand out and a wave of darkfire rippled from around us, pushing the supernaturals within ten yards from us back. "Now!"

Holding my hand, Levi ran up the stairs and I ran with him. The two males who had been in our way stumbled back because of Levi's magic, but as soon as we ran past them, they started after us.

Levi disoriented the two bouncers standing by the double doors, pushed them down the stairs, and locked the doors. "It won't hold for long."

We kept on running, but slowed down once we reached the top of the club. It was more crowded now than when we first arrived.

As we walked by the booths, Levi swiped a leather jacket with a hood and handed it to me. I put it on and pulled the hood over my head to hide my hair. I knew half of the supernaturals here could sense me, but my hair was advertisement enough.

We were halfway to the door when the music stopped. A voice rang out through the speakers. "There's an angel in our midst. Find her!"

Instantly, a dozen supernaturals turned around us.

"Fuck." Levi repeated the same magic from before, but a little stronger, taking people down in a fifteen yard radius. That rippled like dominoes, and more people went down.

Levi and I rushed to the entrance while we were attacked left and right. A tiger shifter lunged at me, its claws poised to swipe at me, but Levi sent a bolt of darkfire to his chest. The shifter landed on a group of witches, who were preparing to hit us.

Then a vampire zoomed into me, holding my shoulder and pulling me back. I elbowed him hard in the chest, but that only made him laugh. Levi threw a bolt of darkfire toward him, making him stagger back a few steps.

Next, a trio of bear shifters stood by the doors.

I prepared to fight them, raising my fists, but Levi was faster. He produced stakes made of darkfire and threw them at their chests, piercing their hearts.

More supernaturals made their way to us, but Levi was able to thwart them with his magic. By the time we burst through the door to the outside, Levi and I were panting. Shouts let us know it wasn't the end yet. Hand in hand, we ran to the opposite side from the hotel, lest we guided them right to where we were hiding.

Thankfully, at this time of the night, Las Vegas's streets were full of tourists and we weaved easily through them. Levi pushed me inside a casino, where he ditched his suit jacket and found me a beige jacket from a chair and a forgotten black baseball hat on a slot machine. I twisted my hair into a bun and hid it under the hat.

When someone opened an "employees only" labeled door, Levi pushed through. "Hey!" the person yelled. "You can't—" Levi zapped his darkfire at the guy and he went down, unconscious.

We ran down the hallway, dodging other employees who shouted we shouldn't be there, until we found an exit door and ran into a back alley. We reached the street and stole a Mercedes from a valet. The guy shouted at us and was definitely calling the police.

"It's fine," Levi told me from behind the wheel. "We'll ditch it in a few blocks."

And we did. We parked the car in an underground garage. After I ditched the beige jacket for a jeans one, and put a black scarf over my hair, Levi and I took the tram the opposite way, toward our hotel.

Carefully, we spied around every corner of the street until we made it to our hotel room.

The moment Levi closed the door, I let out a huge sigh of relief.

We had made it. We were safe, back in the hotel room.

But then my adrenaline hit one last high note as a barrage of other feelings filled me. We hadn't made it.

Everything had gone wrong.

I wasn't one step closer to my wings.

I turned to Levi. "That went well!" I paced in front of him as if the floor was on fire. "The entire place was out to get me the moment we stepped in there. Lars didn't seem interested from the beginning. We didn't secure a meeting with Duncan, the supernaturals in there recognized me, they attacked us, and we had to fight our way out." I halted in front of him. "Oh, wait, you had to fight while I acted like a damsel in distress because I don't have my magic! And it seems I won't have my wings anytime soon either!"

"Listen, sweetheart—"

"You listen!" I jabbed my finger at him. "Why the hell did you quit the negotiations so soon? You could have swayed the man. With your charms and powers, I know you could. And then—"

He loomed over me, almost an entire head taller and as wide as a boulder. "He wanted to buy you."

I let out a hollow chuckle. "That was a lie, a tease."

"It wasn't."

"What?"

"I know he deals in supernatural trafficking, and he's fond of angels."

My mouth fell open. No, it couldn't be. Wait, we were discussing that right now. I was still livid and needed to scream this energy out. "That was beside the point. Who cared if he was serious? You still could have talked him into that meeting."

He stared at me, stoic.

Where was that naughty grin when I needed it? If he was his irritable charming self, I could continue jabbing him, and I would feel better.

I poked on his shoulder. "Come on, say something!"

"You don't want to hear me right now, sweetheart."

"Why not?"

His jaw ticked. "Just drop it."

"I won't." I poked him again. He didn't budge, and let out a long exhale. I poked him again and he closed his eyes. "Fine!" I barked. "If you won't flirt with me or yell back or let me scream this rage away, then I need to burn it off another way." I walked around him.

Levi caught my arm in his big hand. "Where are you going?"

"I need to fight."

"Do you know where to find a cage fight here?"

I narrowed my eyes at him. "How do you know about that?" If I was not mistaken, I had never told him about how I made my living.

"You said you need to fight. I assumed that's what you mean."

Right. "Well, this is Las Vegas. There has to be a fight club somewhere around here and I bet it isn't hard to find." Maybe it would be difficult to secure a match for myself, but probably just getting out of here, walking around searching for the place, and then finding it would be enough to calm me down.

"What the fuck? You're serious?"

"Of course I am. Unless you want to fight me." I raised my fists. "Come on. I bet you can whip my ass, but you can take it slow and let me get some hits in."

Again, he stared at me as if I was weird.

I rolled my eyes at him. "If I can't find a fight club, then I'll go out for a run." I turned back to the door, but then realized my outfit. "I better change—"

"You can't go out, sweetheart."

I placed my hands on my waist. "Says who?"

"We just ran from a club full of supernaturals who were ready to kill you. I bet most of them are still out looking for us. Do you really want to risk meeting them out there?"

Shit, I had not thought of that.

Then fighting with him it was. I kicked my shoes off, walked to the center of the room, pushed the coffee table from the sitting room back, turned to him, and lifted my fists.

"I can't run in here and I can't fight myself." I bounced from side to side. He let out a groan. "Come on, big baddie. Fight me. No magic, though."

"Sweetheart, I won't fight you."

I grabbed a small decorative pillow from the couch and threw it at him. "Fight me." He didn't move. I grabbed another one and threw it at him. "Fight me, or I'll start throwing heavier things." I eyed the decorative vases and knickknacks over the table and counters.

I picked up a small ceramic bowl from the side table and threw it at him. It nicked his shoulder.

Levi let out a hiss.

At first, he didn't do anything else, and I thought I would have to land the first real hit to make him hit me back, but then he ran at me.

Not really expecting it, I froze for a second, and that cost me.

Levi rammed into my middle, pulled me up over his shoulder, and then let me drop on the soft couch. I pushed against him, but he caught my wrists in his hands and secured them above my head. Before I could kick him, he straddled me with his massive body.

I jerked but could barely move an inch.

I stopped, thinking he would let me go so we could have a real fight, but he didn't move. I tugged on my arms; I tried twisting my hips.

"What are you doing?" I jerked some more, trying to get free.

"You want to burn your rage off, sweetheart, then do it. I'll hold you while you thrash and scream like an animal."

I stared at him, appalled. "What?"

He didn't say or do anything. I pulled on my arm, tried lifting my hips, kicking my legs, but it didn't make any difference.

What it did was increase the friction between his body and mine and that certainly reminded me of what had happened in the club. The way we danced together, his possessive hands in mine, his lips on my neck, his breathless whispers in my ear.

Heat spread over my body and I purposely rolled my hips up, knowing I would rub against him, creating more friction.

Levi's brow furrowed. "What are you doing, sweetheart?"

"There's another way you can help me burn this rage, this energy off," I said, my voice husky, unrecognizable.

The blue in his eyes became dark steel as he stared down at me. His jaw ticked and popped; his neck tensed. "You're talking nonsense."

It was like a bucket of freezing water being thrown on my head. What the hell had I suggested? Was I out of my mind? And worse ... he had rejected me.

Was I that unappealing to him? I didn't think I was the prettiest female out there, but I knew I wasn't on the ugly list either. He had called me pretty a few times, and even said I looked stunning earlier this evening. At the club, had it all been pretend? He hadn't felt anything like I did.

My body deflated and I jerked against him, this time careful not to rub my hips on his. "Forget I said anything," I muttered, suddenly embarrassed.

When he didn't let me go, I stopped moving and turned my face, so I was looking at the side of the couch.

Then one of his hands slid from my wrist, around my shoulder, to my rib cage, just underneath my breast. Levi shifted his body over mine, so he wasn't straddling me, but he was perfectly positioned, his hard-on pressed against the apex of my thighs.

He leaned into me, stared into my eyes, and said with a growl, "Just remember you asked for it."

Then he crashed into me.

16

———

No sweet kiss, no tender moment. From the first second, Levi claimed my lips as his and ravaged every inch of my mouth. He sucked on my tongue, making me gasp.

I melted into the delicious, possessive kiss. I didn't think I had ever been kissed like this before, and I couldn't wait to see how the rest would feel.

Meeting his rhythm, I reached up and started undoing the buttons of his shirt. I had seen him shirtless before, and damn, I wanted to touch all of his ripped muscles, to lick them all.

With a growl, Levi broke off the kiss and pulled back. With his desire-filled gaze locked on mine, he wrapped his arms around my waist and rose, taking me with him. He carried me to the dining table, sat me at the edge, ripped his shirt off, and crashed into me again.

This time I was ready for him and when his mouth touched mine, I parted my lips instantly and let him in. I wrapped my legs around his waist, hiking my dress up, and slid my hands over his shoulders and back. By the light, he was so damn hot.

He ground against me, his hard-on creating delicious friction. I moaned, sure he could get me to climax like this.

With a growl, Levi dragged his lips to my jaw and whispered in my ear, "Your sweet scent drives me crazy, sweetheart."

I barely processed his words, lost in the heat of his tongue as it traveled down my neck, licking, sucking, and biting, while he worked the straps of my dress down and around my shoulders. He licked my collarbone and folded the top part of my dress, freeing my breasts.

His tongue drew a line around the top curve of my breast, going around it, and one of his hands closed around the other breast, and pinched the nipple.

He closed his mouth over my other nipple and sucked hard. I cried in pure pleasure and buried my hands in his luscious hair. I saw the hint of a big tattoo curling around the top of his shoulders, but right now, I couldn't care less about a tattoo.

Then he ripped my panties off, knelt in front of me, and put my legs over his shoulders.

Oh, my ...

I felt his hot breath on my thighs and that alone made me shiver.

Levi chuckled. "Is this what you want, sweetheart?"

I groaned, but didn't answer, and that made him chuckle again.

Anticipating what was coming next, I leaned back on my elbows, to give him better access. I knew it, but I wasn't ready. I bucked and cried out when his tongue flicked against my clit.

Levi reached up with one of his hands and played with my breast, while he worked one of his fingers into my entrance. I bucked again. By the light, he had barely started and I was ready.

He slipped a finger inside me and I leaned back fully on the table, unable to hold myself up when I was drowning in pure pleasure.

"So fucking wet," he said before flicking my clit again.

Another finger went in and Levi stopped playing. He moved his tongue around my clit fast and furious, while pumping his fingers inside of me. The fire built up fast and hot, and I could barely control the loud moans coming out of my mouth.

He twisted his fingers, going deeper, and sucked harder on my clit. I didn't try holding back, I didn't want to. I came so hard, I thought I would faint. And Levi kept playing with his tongue a little more, prolonging my climax. I almost sighed in relief when he finally stood up.

Almost.

Looking at me, he licked his fingers. "You taste so good, sweetheart." He reached for the zipper of his pants and stopped. His eyes, so full of desire a second ago, stared back at me with something unreadable. "I don't have a condom."

"It's okay," I said, breathless. "As supernaturals, we are clean, and if you're worried about getting me pregnant, it's fine. Guardians can't get pregnant."

He seemed puzzled by that. "What?"

"Just ... I won't get pregnant." I stretched my legs and wrapped them around his waist. "Now come here."

"As you wish, sweetheart." His half smile was back and he took off his pants. I reached for him, but he flicked his fingers and shadow snakes surged from the sides of the table and wrapped around my wrists, pulling my arms over my head. "That's better."

Levi leaned into me and in one smooth movement, slipped inside me, filling me with his massive hard-on. I gasped, both surprised and amazed by it. Holy shit, he was huge and hot and not gentle at all.

It was fine. I didn't want gentle tonight.

Levi grabbed my waist and started moving fast and hard. One of his hands slid up my stomach and cupped my breast, his fingers playing with my nipple.

"Holy hell, you feel so good," he said with a groan.

He felt so good. He went so deep, touched places I was sure no one had touched before, filled me like no one else had, and I wanted more. Wanting to touch his perfect body, I jerked against the shadow snakes, but they tightened.

He looked at me with his naughty grin. "Tonight, you're mine, sweetheart." He bent over me and took my other breast into his mouth, while pumping non-stop inside me.

Oh, my ... if he kept that up, I would come again.

And I was looking forward to that.

But before I could, Levi pulled back and the snakes disappeared. He grabbed my hand and pulled me up from the table, his intense gaze on mine. He brushed his lips on mine, making me gasp.

Then, he twisted me around, pressed a hand on my back until I folded over the table, my elbows under me, and entered me from behind. I moaned and melted as he somehow went deeper like this and hit different angles, but oh, it felt so damn good.

Levi bent over me, one arm around my waist until it was cupping my breast, and the other on my ass, his fingers digging deep. "So fucking good," he whispered, close to my ear.

He slipped his hand from my ass to my front until his fingers found my clit. I cried out, sure that if the table wasn't underneath me, I would be a puddle on the floor right now.

My stomach tensed; my legs trembled. "Keep going," I whispered.

His fingers moved faster, he thrusted into me harder, his hot breath on my neck ... it was too much.

I came again with a moan.

Levi didn't stop. He kept on thrusting into me. I glanced over my shoulder, I could see he was close, but for some reason, he was holding it.

All right, then, I was taking control.

I pushed him back, until he was off me, and turned around. He looked at me puzzled.

I pressed a finger to his chest, and holding his gaze, pushed him back. He walked backward, trusting me, until he hit the bed in his bedroom. He climbed to the middle of the bed and I climbed over him.

"Holy hell," he said with a groan when I straddled him and took him inside me again.

"My turn," I said with a naughty smile.

He folded his arms around his head and watched me as I moved up and down his erection, slowly at first, but after a few strokes, I wanted more. I needed more.

Slowly, I grazed my nails over the hard planes of his chest and stomach, following the contours of the hundreds of muscles in his torso. How could someone be this ripped? This hot?

I knew we were just fucking, nothing more, but damn, if this didn't feel so good, so right.

I widened my knees and moved fast and hard and deep, taking as much of him inside me as I could, and moaning with each stroke.

"I like seeing you like this, sweetheart," he said, his voice husky. There was something about the way he looked at me, the way he spoke ... I felt the heat, the desire building up inside me again.

He must have felt it, because he reached for me, closed his hands around my waist, and started moving, matching my strokes, and somehow, going even deeper.

"Like that, sweetheart?" he asked.

"Just ... hm ..." I couldn't speak anymore. I was lost in the bliss of the moment.

Levi groaned and I could feel he was close too. His eyes darkened, his hands turned into claws around my waist, and the dark veins covered most of his arms.

It should have scared me, it should have made me stop, but it only made me crazier, more into this moment. He growled, a deep sound that reverberated through his chest.

He closed a claw around my neck and drew me down to him. He captured my mouth with his, his teeth sharp, grazing against my lips as he deepened the kiss, and somehow, making me even more turned on.

I gasped against his lips as I came again!

With another three quick and hard thrusts, Levi groaned and came too. I melted on top of him, both of us trembling uncontrollably.

His arms, back to their human form, closed around me, and it felt so good, so warm, so right. Bliss and exhaustion found me and suddenly, I could barely keep my eyes open. I rolled to Levi's side, snuggled closed to his warm body, hugged a pillow, and fell deep asleep.

17

I STIRRED IN BED, FALLING DOWN FROM SLEEP BLISS, AND THEN froze.

By the light, I was in Levi's bedroom, completely naked, and wrapped in his bed sheets.

I spied from under my lashes.

Of course, the other side of the bed was empty.

What had I expected? I had to remember Levi was a demon, and not a nice one, and what we had done last night, even though it had been surreal and the mere thought of it tightened my thighs and made me hot all over, it had been a one-time thing. It had been an exercise to relieve the stress and rage we both were feeling.

Nothing more.

Now that that was out of our system, we could go on as if nothing had happened.

And he was already ahead of the game.

I sat up, holding the sheets over my chest, and listened. Nothing. Levi was either being quiet, or he wasn't in the hotel room.

If it weren't for the bond that pulled him toward me, I was certain he would have left already. Probably long ago.

With a sigh, I got up, grabbed a robe from his bathroom, tied it around myself, and paused at the bedroom's door. I opened it, spied out into the common room. Yup, no sign of him. I felt both relaxed and worried about that. Where had he gone? Did he think it was a promising idea to be out there after what happened at the club last night?

Well, he was a grown demon. He knew what he was doing.

I hoped.

I crossed the common room into my bedroom—the bed untouched—and went directly to the bathroom, where I took a long, hot shower. After, I put on black leggings, a burgundy tank top, and left my leather jacket and my combat boots by the bed.

Another twenty minutes passed and I paced the communal area, worried. What if someone had found Levi? A demon or a bear shifter, and now—

I stopped those thoughts. No, Levi was powerful. He had been able to get us out of a full nightclub. He could get away from a handful of demons if attacked.

Damn, I couldn't sit still, so I picked up my phone and called him.

The door opened and Levi walked in—his phone vibrating in one hand, a brown bag in the other, and a small box wedged under his arm.

"Good morning, sweetheart," he said, the lopsided grin on full display. "Worried about me?"

I almost winced.

All right. We were playing the last-night-didn't-happen game, then.

"What do you have there?" My tone wasn't as natural as his. He was probably used to one-night stands, but I wasn't.

He set the brown bag on the small table—the table he had spread me over and …

I shook my head, pushing those thoughts away.

I focused on the bag and I saw it was from a diner.

"Breakfast," Levi said, his voice tight. He placed the box on the counter that made up the kitchen. "And this … is a surprise."

I frowned. Coming from him, I wasn't so sure I liked surprises. Opening the bag, I got two coffee cups set in a holder, and two hot breakfast sandwiches. We sat down across from each other, and once again, it was hard not to remember what that table had been used for last night.

"What now?" I asked to occupy my mind. I needed something new to focus on. "What do we do?" I took a bite of my sandwich.

"This is where this comes in." He pointed to the box. "It's a fake witch's wand."

The wheels in my mind worked. Wands were rare and only the most powerful witches of certain covens had them. "This could interest Duncan."

He nodded. "Enough to let us in his house."

I frowned. "That's a big if."

"I know, but it's all we got." He sipped his coffee.

"How did you get it?" I asked, curious.

"I had a friend of mine make it and send it to me."

A friend of his. I couldn't see Levi with friends, just a bunch of people who owed him favors. "Okay, let's say he invites us in because of the wand and I find my wings. Then what? We fight our way out? I bet someone like him has lots of lackeys."

Levi set his coffee down. "He does, and that's why I called mine." I stared at him and he elaborated. "I called a dozen demons that work for me. They are coming to help us." He showed me his dazzling grin. "Don't worry, sweetheart, we'll get your wings back."

I wanted to believe him, but after what happened in the nightclub last night, I had my doubts about if we would be invited to Duncan's because of a wand. He sounded like he was picky about the items he collected.

We ate the rest of our sandwiches in an awkward silence, which obviously made me overanalyze everything.

Including admiring how sturdy this table was.

"You said something last night," Levi started, his voice atypically serious. "That angels couldn't get pregnant, but you didn't elaborate on that."

I drank the last sip of my coffee, then stared at him. "It's not all female angels. Only the ones who graduate from Guardian Academy and follow the ranks."

"Why?"

"So, the females can focus solely on their missions and the safety of all angels and humans, not just their kids."

Levi's brows curled down. "You graduate and your gift is to have your body mutilated?"

"It isn't as barbaric as that. It's done with magic, but hm, yeah, our ovaries are blocked and we can't get pregnant. It's for the best," I repeated the words I had heard throughout my life.

Any female accepted into the academy knew that once they went down that path, if they graduated and wanted to become a guardian, then they had to go through the procedure before joining the Cherubin.

"How about exceptions?" Levi asked. "There are always exceptions."

I shook my head. "No exception." In the centuries this procedure was performed, I hadn't heard or read of any exceptions.

"That sounds barbaric. And I thought angels were righteous and good."

"We are," I almost shouted. Then I cleared my throat and tried again. "We are. It's a hard choice we have to make, a selfless one. We choose the safety and well-being of others above our own interests."

"You're okay with never being a mother?"

I shifted on my chair. Honestly, I avoided thinking about the topic, since I knew it wasn't on the table for me. "Yes."

"You're not a good liar, sweetheart."

"Neither are you," I retorted, getting worked up. "You pretend to be this big, bad demon, but you are kind and caring when it comes to your sister and Heidi. What is it? Which one is the real you?"

His jaw ticked and I knew I had hit a nerve. "Both, sweetheart. I can care for my sister and Heidi, who was like a mother to us, and still be the biggest evil you've ever met."

I almost laughed in his face. I had helped my friends defeat the Shadow Fae King from the fae realm, warlocks and vampires who were intent on taking other supernaturals' powers to create a super weapon, and a prince of the underworld ... who had taken my magic in the process. But he was now dead.

While I had become practically a human.

I had met real evil.

Levi wasn't good by any means, but he was far from the biggest evil out there.

"If you say so," I mumbled.

"What was that, sweetheart?"

With a groan, I stood. "All right. You got the wand and will try to set up a meeting with Duncan. So, you're going to call him?"

He stared at me for a minute, his tension still visible in his expression. He exhaled through his nose and his face relaxed. He leaned back in his chair, all charm again. "I won't call him, sweetheart. I'll have my demons call his demons. Meanwhile, we'll be going to San Francisco."

"When are we leaving?"

He pushed to his feet. "Now."

18

Levi thought it was a clever idea to change cars again, so this time, he rented a sports Mercedes for us. It was more luxurious than the SUV, but it was smaller.

Couldn't the man rent something simpler? A car like this caught a lot of attention and that was exactly what we didn't need. But I didn't say anything, because even though he was acting charming and cocky, I could see it was a mask and he was irritated. Or maybe furious.

My mind came up with three hundred scenarios about why he could be furious, despite my efforts to forget about him for a few minutes at least.

One, he was still mad at me because of the bond and being forced to come and help me. I mean, why wouldn't he be? I certainly would. But in the last couple of days, I thought he wasn't as mad anymore ... maybe something I said or did triggered the feelings again.

Two, I had felt turned on last night, which in turn made him turned on, since he felt what I felt, and that was why he slept with me. Because I wanted him to, and he couldn't help it. But the truth was, he hadn't wanted it and now despised me for it.

Three, I stepped on his toes, or elbowed his ribs, or something? I didn't know. Honestly, with how moody he was behaving, it could be anything, really.

The first leg of the drive was quiet and tense. I ignored Levi, turned to the window, and tried napping. But I couldn't. My mind was too agitated.

Last night, running from the nightclub, it had been crazy. This morning when leaving the hotel, I thought we would encounter a supernatural or a dozen, who were lurking around the town, still searching for us.

Thankfully, no one was waiting, and we left Las Vegas behind without any trouble.

Around one in the afternoon, we stopped for lunch at a diner outside Bakersfield. We were getting closer to San Francisco, and I was getting nervous.

Soon, I would be within walking distance from my wings.

I was afraid of my reaction when I saw them. I was afraid in what state I would find them. Were they part of a pretty display, or were they ripped feather by feather?

My heart lurched in pain.

Levi looked up from the menu. "What was that, sweetheart?"

Shit, he had felt it. I set my menu down and stared at him seated across the booth. "Just thinking about my wings."

"That's—"

The server appeared then and took our orders—two cheeseburgers, fries, and Cokes. Simple, fast. We wanted to get going as soon as possible.

When she was gone, Levi opened his mouth to say something, but his phone rang.

"Yes?" he answered it. He listened for a few seconds. "Get me his direct number. I'll call him myself." He turned it off and fumed at the screen.

"What is it?"

"Duncan's people said he's not interested in a wand."

I frowned. "I thought he wouldn't be. We'll need to think of something else."

Levi tilted his head and locked his baby blues on me. "If only we had something, an object, maybe a weapon, a powerful dagger or sword or stake. Maybe he would fall for that."

I averted my eyes.

I knew of such a weapon. I had hidden such a weapon, but no one other than Molraz and Rhodes knew that. Unless Rhodes had told Elysium that I had stolen it.

I grabbed the butter knife on the table. "Perhaps we can find a witch who can glamour this and infuse it with some power, enough to fool a demon."

He kept staring at me, so intent. "Witches can't glamour things, sweetheart. That's for fae."

I knew that, but I wouldn't correct it now, lest he thought I was hiding something.

The server came back with our food, and we ate in silence. Halfway through the meal, I remembered Levi was about to say something before we ordered our meal, and then we both forgot.

I was about to ask him what it was, when two guys entered the diner, staring at me. I couldn't pinpoint what exactly they were, but I was sure they weren't humans.

I stiffened.

"What is it, sweetheart?" Levi followed my gaze. "A half demon, and a lion shifter."

The duo sat three booths from us. The server came, they ordered coffee, and all the while, they kept shooting glances our way.

Could they have been at the nightclub last night? We were over four hours from Las Vegas, and it was another day. Those supernaturals had either forgotten about Levi and me, or they were still looking for us around Las Vegas.

They wouldn't be out here. Right?

Levi's phone rang again and he cursed under his breath. "Yes?" he answered with a bite.

Three seconds in and he stared at me, eyes narrowed. He kept listening to whoever was on the other line, and his gaze shifted to the supernatural duo, the ones who were still shooting daggers with their eyes.

"Understood," Levi said before putting his phone down.

He looked out the window, to a pickup truck that had parked in front of the diner, bringing in more supernaturals.

My stomach coiled. "What's going on?"

"Apparently, the angels went crazy," he said, his voice low. "They put out something like a wanted poster of you. Extremely high reward."

"What?" I squeaked.

I had never heard of anything like that before. It was insane!

Then my phone rang. I frowned, since only a handful of people had this number. It was Hazel. Surely, she had seen the "poster" and the reward. I ignored the call, but soon my phone vibrated with lots of messages.

"We need to get out of here," Levi said.

My frown deepened. Yeah, we had to, but I didn't have my powers. Other than fighting my way out, I was a sitting duck. "Lead the way," I mumbled, irritated with this shit.

Casually, Levi left a one-hundred-dollar bill on the table and stood up. I drank the last sip of my drink and stood with him. As we expected, the two supernaturals stood and the ones outside formed a wide semicircle in front of the front door.

Levi slipped his hand in mine. "Ready?" he asked, his voice low.

He lifted one hand and shadows jutted out from all corners, enveloping the diner in darkness. Levi pulled me down and we rushed to the kitchen—I went with him, because I couldn't see anything, but perhaps he could; after all, this was his magic.

We crossed the kitchen—the scent of grease thick in the air—and exited through the back. The shadows covered most of the building and some of the parking lot, but when we finally stepped through the dark cloud into a gravel space in the back, four supernaturals were waiting for us.

"You didn't think it would be easy, right?" one of them asked. From what I could tell, he was a lesser demon. His companions were two vampires, and a shifter, not sure what kind.

"Where's the fun in easy?" Levi asked, his tone as charming as ever.

He sent out a wave of darkfire. The two vampires zoomed out of range, but the magic hit the demon and the shifter. They went down but didn't stay down. Levi kept assailing them with his magic. The lesser demon threw his darkfire at Levi, and the shifter shifted into a lion and lunged.

I turned to the side, with the idea of trying to get the car, any car, so we could get away from him, but faced the two vampires.

"Sweet, sweet angel," one of them said.

Shit.

I brought my fists up, but they were too fast for me. They played with me as if I was nothing. I punched, jabbed, and kicked air, while they zoomed around me and karate-chopped my back, my neck, and my stomach, taking the air away.

Dizzy, I fell to my knees. One vampire caught my hair and pulled my head back, exposing my throat, while the other loomed over me, licking his lips.

"I bet her blood tastes sweet."

"We shouldn't taste it. We have a reward to get."

"I won't bite her. I'll do this." He ran a nail over my neck. A slow stinging pain spread where he had touched. Then, he brought his fingers to his mouth and moaned. "Delicious."

"That's enough," a fae said as he approached us. I didn't know what kind he was, but he sounded like the boss.

I blinked, trying to focus enough to get my bearings. More supernaturals arrived and formed a semicircle around us. Levi had already killed the first two, but now he was busy with another handful of enemies.

"Just take her," the fae said.

No, they couldn't take me. If they took me, they would lock me in a room until the angels came for me, and as an almost human, I would have no way to escape.

I pushed to my feet, finally landed a good uppercut on the vampire, and a back kick on the other.

The fae moved his fingers and vines sprouted from under the gravel and wrapped around my legs and arms. "I'll enjoy this," he said. Then, he punched my gut and my chin.

I blacked out for a moment.

When I came to, I was too far gone, my head and my chest hurt, I couldn't breathe and could barely see, but I knew I was on the shoulder of one of the vampires, and they were taking me away.

Suddenly, a roar erupted in the air.

I forced myself to stay conscious, to find out what that was.

Levi, in his demon form, barreled into the supernaturals.

He picked up a car as if it weighed as much as a feather and threw it at three of them, enveloped three in his shadows and they seemed to be suffocating, and he flapped his wings and arched into the sky, landing right in front of us.

He shocked the fae and the vampires with his darkfire and caught me in his arms before I fell to the ground. Without wasting a second, Levi took off running to the woods.

"Hang on. I'll call for help," he said, his voice monstrous.

I blinked, trying to look at him. I could feel he was in his demon form, but it was still his scent, still his warmth. I rested my head on his shoulder. "Just hold on to me," I whispered.

Then, I fainted.

19

My head pounded and I hadn't even opened my eyes.

By the light, what had happened—

Before the sentence finished forming in my mind, I remembered. The diner, the price on my head, the supernaturals, the fight.

Levi running with me in his arms.

I sat up and groaned as the pain intensified. I inhaled a handful of times, until the pain lessened. Then I opened my eyes and found myself lying on a bedsheet on a torn couch in a dark, strange room. There were a couple of windows to my right, but they had been covered with plywood, and two metal doors ahead.

Beside the couch was a cardboard box with my phone, a water bottle, and one vial of my potion. Right, I didn't even remember when the last time was I had taken it. I tipped it and drank a good dose. Then I grabbed my phone.

This couldn't be right. It was almost eleven in the morning, which meant ... I had passed out for almost a full day.

My phone also had dozens of messages—mostly from

Hazel, one of the only numbers I had saved, and another unknown number, but when I clicked on the messages, I saw it was from Khalisa.

I had been right. They had heard the angels had put a price on my head and they were worried. Hazel also told me all of my friends were desperate after me. They wanted to know what was going on and what they could do to help me.

My heart squeezed.

If I told them the truth, would they believe in me, or would they side with Elysium?

I sighed and tried forgetting about it. I wouldn't contact them; I wouldn't even answer Hazel's and Khalisa's messages. Thankfully, I hadn't given Erin my number when we met a couple of days ago, or I'm sure she would be calling me too.

The less they knew, the better.

Where was Levi?

I walked to the doors. I opened one. It squeaked loudly and I found a smaller room with one thin window near the ceiling, and several empty and broken shelves along the walls. A storage room?

I opened the other one and found a dark and wide corridor with a handful of doors. I searched for a switch on the wall, since this corridor had no windows and the doors were all closed, but when I found it, it didn't work.

"Levi?" I called.

Nothing.

Using the flashlight from my phone, I started down the corridor and tried every single door. Four of them were locked, and only the last one wasn't.

I pushed the door open, this time silent, and stepped into a wide room with a vaulted ceiling. It looked like an abandoned plant equipped with broken assembly lines and empty crates.

In the center of the room a figure was tied to a metal column, much like the first demon I had seen in Houston.

But this time it wasn't a demon.

It was an angel.

My blood went cold, and Levi, who had been looming over the beaten angel, turned to me.

He straightened and put his game face on. "Awake, sweetheart?"

I snapped out of my stupor and marched to him, anger boiling in my veins. "What the hell are you doing?"

"I snatched one of the angels who were after you, sweetheart." He dared to sound proud! "You're a Cherubin, right? I think he's a Cherubin."

I glanced at the angel, and a quick wave of relief coursed through me when I didn't recognize him. Not that it made this better, but at least I wouldn't be facing a former friend.

The angel groaned, his eyes half closed and unseeing. He had silver-blond hair cut short, fair skin, but that was all I could make out of his features underneath the bruises on his face. His body was slumped forward, and if it weren't for the magical ropes, he would be passed out on the floor.

If I had to guess, I would say he had probably graduated from Guardian Academy not long ago, and the pitiful thing had already been captured by an evil demon and beaten to a pulp.

"You shouldn't have done that," I snarled.

"Why not? They are hunting you, sweetheart. I need to know all of the details so I can protect you, and the only way to do that was to get one of them."

While I was passed out on that filthy couch, Levi had hunted the angels.

It was sickening.

"If he's a Cherubin," and he looked like one, "he probably doesn't know anything! He's a grunt the higher levels order around. You got an innocent angel, my kind, and you're just letting your anger out!"

Levi scoffed. "There are no innocent angels, sweetheart."

"What the hell are you implying? That I'm as bad as they are saying?"

"Maybe you are."

"Do you even hear yourself?"

"I didn't change, sweetheart. You're the one who pretended not to hear me, not to see me, for the past few days."

I flinched.

That was it. Maybe I had seen only what I wanted to see and ignored the rest. Because a person, or a demon, with a sliver of good in his heart, wouldn't be doing this to another being, no matter how evil they were.

"Let him go," I said, my tone definite. "Untie him and let him go."

"So he can bring his friends back here? I don't think so."

"Then blindfold him, take him somewhere out of the way, and then run." I paused, the words all rushing to my tongue. I needed to choose them right. "But then, please, let him go."

"Can't do that, sweetheart. You see, this angel isn't innocent and—"

I groaned. "Holy shit, stop!"

Levi's eyes hardened. "If you don't want to see me work, sweetheart, you're welcome to go."

"I might just—"

"Ariella," the angel croaked.

I stilled for three seconds, shocked, and then turned to him. "Yes. I'm here." I wanted to reach for him, to help him stand straighter, but I was afraid that wherever I touched him, it would hurt. "Are you okay? Can I get you anything?"

Stupid questions, but they blurted out of my mouth.

The angel lifted his head and fixed his eyes on mine. His mouth quivered, his shoulder shook, and I thought he was crying. Until his mouth contorted in a big smile and he laughed.

I took a step back.

"We've been searching everywhere for you, angel-killer," the angel said, his voice raspy. "The guardians will find you, they will capture you, and they will ki—"

Levi punched the angel's face, the sound of a crack echoing through the place. I gasped and startled back.

But the angel laughed and faced us again, his cheekbone clearly broken. "And you, Leviathan, are going down with her." He smiled at me, blood in his teeth. "We were told you had sided with demons. Now I have proof."

Levi grabbed his hair and pulled his head up. "Answer me, you motherfucker. Who sent you? Who is spreading lies about Ariella?"

Lies? Levi believed me.

"No one is lying," the angel said. "She betrayed her kind and killed a dozen angels. The entirety of Elysium knows about it."

My stomach twisted in knots. I knew every angel in Elysium must have heard about it, must have believed it, because why wouldn't they when the famous, powerful Archangel Rhodes told them so?

But to think my mother and my sister believed them too ... that made me sick.

I frowned. "It's not true."

"If it's not true, then why don't you face us? Why don't you bring the dagger and turn yourself in?" the angel asked. I froze at the mention of the dagger and Levi glanced at me, eyes narrowed. "We are good, righteous beings. We would give you a fair trial and—"

Levi closed his hand around the angel's throat, squeezing it. "You just said you'll capture her and kill her. That she's done for. I don't hear anything about a fair trial in that statement."

The angel smiled, even though it had to be hurting. "You're smart for a demon."

I pressed a hand to my stomach.

This angel ... he wasn't behaving like an angel. He wasn't good and righteous. He was calculating and almost as evil as a demon.

"Who sent you? What do you know about me?" The words blurted out from my lips before I could stop them. I pressed a hand to my mouth in horror. "No, no, no." I took two steps back. "I'm not doing this."

I glanced at Levi. He didn't seem one bit worried about this, about my feelings. It looked like a fun game for him.

And it made me sick.

I turned and ran.

"Ariella!" Levi called after me.

"There's nowhere to run, traitor!" the angel shouted. "We'll find you and—" He groaned as Levi landed a hit on him.

I didn't stop to look; I didn't want to be a witness to this anymore.

Before I left the room, a hand closed around my arm and pulled me back. "Ariella, you have to understand—"

I faced him. "There's nothing to understand. You're a demon. This is what you do. But ..." I sucked in a sharp breath. I didn't want to be a part of this, I couldn't. "Let me go."

"You shouldn't be out there by yourself." He sounded mad and that didn't help his cause. "It's dangerous."

I jerked my arm free. "What do you care? Are you afraid of getting hurt if I do?"

"Sweetheart—"

I screamed. "Let me go!" I pulled on my arm again, and this time I got free. "And don't come after me!"

20

DESPERATION CLAWED INSIDE MY CHEST AS I RAN OUT OF THE building into a deserted parking lot and cloudy skies. I inhaled deeply, trying to cleanse my mind. I wanted to forget it, pretend I had never seen it.

If I still had my magic, I would have fought Levi, immobilized him, and freed the angel. But as it was, I wasn't strong enough to fight, and if I tried to free the angel with brute force, Levi would overpower me.

I did what any coward would do. I walked away.

The building, clearly now an abandoned plant, was lonely on a rural road in the middle of nowhere. I pulled up my phone and checked the map app—we were around Lost Hills, California

Following the road, a couple of miles down, there was a small town.

I glanced at the car in the parking lot. Apparently, while I was out, Levi hadn't just captured an angel. He had gone back to the diner and retrieved the car with our stuff.

I could take the car and go to the small town ... and do what?

I didn't know.

All I knew was that being near Levi was giving me whiplash. One second, he was sweet and charming, and I could almost see the goodness in him. The next, he was a demon.

It was confusing and scary.

I could go, but what good would that do? Because of the damn bond, I would make Levi suffer and he would have to follow me.

Unless I broke the bond.

I still didn't have my wings and my revenge, but I knew the collector's name, I knew where he lived. I could get there by myself.

How would I get my wings back? I had no idea, but I was certain I could figure something out.

I unlocked my phone and called Hazel.

She answered in two rings. "Ariella, holy shit, finally! I was so worried."

I frowned. We had lots of friends in common, but Hazel barely knew me. Why did she care?

"I'm okay," I said, my voice tight. "I'm guessing you saw the reward."

"Unless a coven or a pack is hiding from the world, the entire supernatural society saw it." She sighed. "Your friends are losing their minds trying to find you. I confess I almost gave them your number, but I thought you wouldn't want me to."

"You did well. I don't want to talk to them. Thank you."

"Though, Ariella, I have to ask: What happened? Why are they after you?"

"I ... I don't want to talk about that. Would you just believe me if I told you whatever they are saying, it's not true? I'm innocent, I promise."

"I believe you. And for the record, they aren't saying much. Just that you committed a grave crime and you need to be captured ASAP."

"Captured? Not killed on sight?"

"No." She paused. "Why would they kill you?"

"To silence me." I cursed under my breath. "I've already said too much, and I'm putting you at risk by calling."

"But you called for a reason. What can I do for you?"

"Have you figured out how to break the bond? Between Levi and me?"

"I have! It shouldn't be too hard to break it." I heard the shuffle of papers. "I wrote a list of ingredients down, but there's one thing: You'll need a witch to perform the ritual."

"Shit," I muttered.

"I mean, I can try to modify the spell and you can try to do it yourself, but without a witch's magic, I'm not sure it'll work."

I would need Lacey for this.

"Just tell me the two versions, I'll figure something out."

"Okay. I'll take a picture of the list and send it to you. I'll also text you the instructions. If you have any questions, you know where to find me."

"That sounds great. Thanks."

"And, Ariella ... if you need anything, not just for this spell, but for any other trouble you're in, I'm here. Your friends are here. I know that if you called them, they wouldn't hesitate in helping you, no matter what."

I knew that too, but I really didn't want them involved in this mess.

"Thanks," was all I said before I turned off the call.

A second later, my phone dinged with a picture and a short text of instructions.

Perfect.

I stashed my phone in my pocket and turned to the car.

I was so out of here.

AT FIRST, I DROVE TO THE SMALL TOWN. I WANTED TO PUT AS much distance between Levi and me as I could, even if that caused him pain. He deserved it.

Then I searched on my phone where I could find all the ingredients for the spell. Thankfully, it was nothing too crazy and I found most of it in a tea and candle shop, a garden supply shop, and a grocery store.

Finally, around five in the afternoon, I stopped by a quaint coffee shop and got me a caramel latte and two blueberry muffins—I hadn't eaten since yesterday and I was starving!

All the while, I had my hair tied in a low bun and a baseball cap we had gotten in Vegas over my face. I also bought a pair of cheap sunglasses at the grocery store and wore them even when inside.

Now with the entire supernatural world after me, I had to be extra careful. That was why, after getting my food, I didn't stay at the coffee shop. I drove to the nearest park—a corner field with a playground, half a basketball court, and a skate ramp—and sat on a stone bench under a tree.

There were a handful of people in the park, but from what I could tell, none of them were supernaturals.

I was fine for now.

I tried to keep my mind clear as I ate, lest my thoughts spoil the food, but once I was done, I couldn't help it anymore. I needed to figure out what to do now.

I would go back to Levi, ask Lacey to join us, and break the bond. Of course, he wouldn't protest. In fact, he would be glad since he then could get rid of me. We would perform the ritual, I would ask him to drop me off at the nearest train or bus station, and then both of us would go on our merry ways.

And somewhere in there, I would free the angel he had captured.

Perfect.

Then why did I feel such a deep hole inside my chest?

I stood, ready to go back, when the hair on my arms stood on end. I turned and found the source: a group of supernaturals on the other side of the park, looking for something.

Or someone.

Shit, they had found me. The angels had probably announced my last-known location, and supernaturals in all directions had been looking for me.

I lowered my head and hurried to the car.

I heard a chilling howl from behind me, then some growls and grumbles.

A force slammed into my side and pushed me against a thick tree, shadows forming around me. A hand closed over my mouth, while a powerful body pressed against mine, keeping me in place.

I stared at Levi's face, so damn close, his intent blue eyes locked on mine.

"Stay still," he whispered against my ear. "They smelled you but didn't see you." He lowered his hand from my mouth and shifted his murderous gaze to the supernaturals as they came this way. "My shadows will confuse them."

I remained still, my mind and body divided between the panic of being found and having to fight again, and the warmth of Levi's figure against mine. The way his heavy breathing moved his chest and it touched mine. How his thick leg was wedged between my thighs, keeping me in place. His strong neck so close to my nose and his delicious musk scent fogging my mind.

This wasn't right. He was a demon, an evil one. I had to keep reminding myself of that.

The incredible night we shared, how hot he was, had nothing to do with this. I couldn't let it get into my head, in my body, in my veins.

Levi adjusted himself, pressing more of his body against mine, his breathing heavy against my ear, his lips touching my jaw.

"Those feelings aren't appropriate for this moment, sweetheart," he whispered, his voice husky.

By the light.

"She isn't here," a voice said and I froze.

Levi lifted his head and then I could see. About seven supernaturals walking a few feet from us, looking all around, and yet, they couldn't see us.

"Her scent was stronger here a few minutes ago," one of them said.

"It was, but she's gone," another one said.

"Let's spread out," a third one suggested. "She can't be far."

They walked away. One of them stopped right beside the car, which was enveloped in shadows too, but he couldn't see it. Levi and I remained still and hidden, while the supernaturals fanned out and disappeared.

Finally, the shadows disappeared and Levi stepped away

from me. He rubbed his chest. "Do you have any idea of the pain you caused me, sweetheart?"

I had, and it had been on purpose. Seriously, I wasn't in the mood to talk to him. All I wanted was to get to the car, drive somewhere safe, perform the ritual, and break the bond before other demons came after me to claim their prize.

A lightbulb went off in my head and I stared at Levi, my eyes wide. "I know how to get Duncan to invite us to his house."

21

LEVI CROSSED HIS ARMS AND STARED AT ME. "AND HOW IS that?"

"Offer myself."

He blinked, as if he hadn't heard me right. Then his eyes darkened. "You're insane."

"Why? Doesn't he collect rare items? What's rarer than a powerless angel who's being hunted by the entire world? He's probably heard about me too; he knows I'm valuable. He'd probably love to lock me away in his art gallery." Or wherever it was he displayed his collection.

"Sweetheart, do you really think he'll do that and buy himself a fight against the angels?"

Shit, I hadn't thought about that. "Perhaps not, but if he's a real collector, he would love to take a look at me, even if for only a minute. That would be enough to grant us entry into his house."

I had gone nuts. Here I was, coming up with a plan to continue working with Levi, when a minute ago, I was willing to break the bond and let him go.

But I needed him. If this worked, then I could definitely break the bond after. He would be free of me; I would be free of him ... no harm, no foul.

"I hear you, sweetheart, and I agree it isn't a bad plan, but ..." He glanced around. "Can we talk about this somewhere else? We shouldn't be out in the open like this."

At least he was right about that.

We walked to the car, he hopped behind the wheel, I took the passenger seat, and then we were on the road again.

"Where are we going?" I asked, as the scenery changed and we merged onto the interstate.

"There are demons everywhere around here. We need to keep moving."

It made sense, of course. And the fact that he was going northwest, toward San Francisco, told me he was considering my proposition.

Then I remembered. "What about the angel? We didn't go back for him."

"He's not our concern anymore."

"What do you mean?" I gasped. "Did you kill him?"

Levi's jaw popped, his eyes narrowed on the road. "He's gone."

By the light, Levi had killed the angel.

I couldn't believe it. I wanted to punch him, to strangle him, but I restrained myself. I pushed down on my anger and resentment for now. If my plan succeeded, I would soon be free of him, and nobody else would have to get hurt.

I sank into my seat, fighting tears, and ended up falling asleep. I woke up almost one hour later when we passed a drive-thru and got ourselves dinner. We found a motel off the road that had a main building with several single rooms and cabins around a stone path just behind it.

Levi got us the key for one of the cabins. It was quite charming with a gas fireplace and rustic decorations, though it wasn't much better than the single rooms, since it had just one bed.

Levi saw me staring at the bed. "Don't worry, sweetheart, I'll take the couch."

My cheeks heated up and I was sure he felt whatever I was feeling—even I couldn't place it. My feelings for him were so messed up. We had started with me hating his guts, then he grew on me, we had shared one amazing night of hot sex, and now he was back to being evil and me to despising him.

And yet ... No. I shook my head and forced myself to forget everything else. Right now, Levi was a temporary business partner. That was all. No feelings or past involved.

"Can we talk about my plan now?" I asked as we unwrapped our burgers.

"I would rather eat without losing my temper, sweetheart."

I frowned. So, he wasn't considering it? Or that was him acknowledging that this was a sensitive topic, and he would really listen to me later.

So, we ate in tense silence. It was awkward and I wanted to say something to break this tension, but why? Didn't I just tell myself that Levi was my business associate, nothing else. I didn't need to fraternize with him. All I needed was for him to agree to my plan.

If it all worked out, I could have my wings tomorrow night. Just the thought made me feel lighter. With a new bounce to my step, I took a quick shower, changed into black leggings and my sleep shirt—I wouldn't be pantless again near him—and sat down on the bed.

I watched as Levi paced in front of the fireplace.

"Aren't you going to take a shower?" I asked.

He shook his head. "Later."

"Then ... can we talk now? Or are you busy brooding?"

He stopped and turned his frown at me. "There's nothing to talk about."

I stood. "What do you mean? You promised we would talk about my plan."

"I didn't promise anything, sweetheart. I said we would talk later to get you out of there."

"What?" I almost shouted. "What the hell?" I started after him. "You—"And I bumped into an invisible wall. I almost fell back, but bumped into the bed, and was able to find my balance. I reached forward and felt it. "What is this? What did you do?"

"I can't have you doing something stupid, sweetheart." Levi moved the couch three inches to the side and I saw it— the lines of the circle he had drawn around the bed and part of the cabin.

Rage bloomed in my veins. "You did what?!" I banged against the wall, but it was to no avail. Maybe if I had my magic, but without it ... I was as useless as a human. There was nothing I could do against the simplest witch or demon circles. "Levi, get me out of there right now!"

"I can't do that, sweetheart."

"What, then? You're holding me so you can hand me over to the angels yourself?"

Levi walked up to the circle, just out of reach. "I'm doing this for your own good, sweetheart—"

"Don't sweetheart me!" I yelled as loud as I could. "You asshole! Let me go, damn it!"

"Hate me all you want," he said with a growl. "You'll thank me later."

He spun on his heels and walked out of the cabin.

I shouted his name, screamed, threw the side lamp at him, only to have it bounce off the magical wall and break on the floor.

Desperation suffocated me. How could I get away from here? From this?

The truth was, I couldn't.

***

NOW I UNDERSTOOD WHY LEVI HAD FED ME AND WAITED UNTIL I took a shower to lock me in the circle—because he didn't come back that night.

I called his phone, but he didn't answer. At some point, my phone died and the charger was on the other side of the circle.

Bored and angry, I lay down on the bed and ended up sleeping.

I woke up early and realized he had come back in the middle of the night: now the circle had an adjacent one that included the bathroom.

At least he had thought about that ...

No, he wasn't getting any sympathy from me.

How much more would he have to do for me to remember he was a vicious demon? Shortly after I first met him, he killed a demon who had been his captive. After that, he would have allowed demons to kill innocent humans, if it weren't for the Blackthorn Hunters showing up at the park. He had captured and tortured an angel, and now he had trapped me in here against my will.

And according to him, he was going after my wings.

I wondered. Would he give them back to me, or would he sell them? Maybe add that to the angels' offer and get a larger reward?

At this point, I couldn't discount anything from him.

It was the middle of the morning when the cabin door opened and I opened my mouth to yell at him—but Lacey was the one walking toward me.

I swallowed the words, their taste turning my mouth sour. "Lacey?" I was confused. "What are you doing here?"

"Oh, Ariella." She halted right outside the circle. "I'm so sorry. My stupid brother—"

"Whatever you're saying about me, you can stop." Levi walked in, a white bag and a cup of coffee in his hands. He stared at me with his lopsided grin. "Good morning, sweetheart."

If I could, I would punch him.

"What's going on?" I asked, and then I remember why she had stayed behind. "Shouldn't you be with Heidi?"

"She's much better," she said. "I was thinking about leaving when Levi called me."

"Wait. Are you in on this?" I thought Lacey wasn't as bad as her brother.

He reached inside the circle and placed the cup and the brown bag on the floor. "I can't leave you alone while I go retrieve your wings, so I asked my sister to come babysit you."

"For the record, he asked for help. He didn't give me any specifics until I got here." She shot him a glare. "He knows I'm against this."

He held her stare. "And I told her she either behaves, or she'll join you inside that circle."

Lacey stood still, clearly afraid of her brother. "I'll behave," she said softly.

"Good." He turned his smile at me again. "Now if you'll excuse me, I have a break-in to plan."

"There's an easier way to do this," I told him.

His smile faltered for half a second. "I'll be back later." He gave one last warning glance at his sister, then he walked out.

I opened my mouth, but Lacey held her finger over her puckered lips.

She counted to ten before going to the window and spying from under the curtains. "He's leaving." She rushed back to me. "Holy cow, I thought he was joking when he told me he had trapped you." She shook her head. "He can be so stubborn."

"Stubborn?" I scoffed. "He's evil. Terrible. I'm disgusted and appalled, and I want to get out of here now!"

Lacey pulled an armchair close to the circle and sat down. "Tell me what happened."

I crossed my arms and didn't say a word. What if all of this was a game? What if she was helping him?

But that wasn't it, was it? Lacey was different. Levi had protected her from their father, from his evil fate. He had sent her away so she wouldn't turn out like him.

So, I sat down on the floor, grabbed the breakfast I was brought, and I told her. Not everything—I didn't tell her how we danced at the nightclub, and what happened when we got to the hotel—but I told her all the rest.

"I ... I don't even know what to say." Her shoulders were down and her voice low. "Our father is evil. He might not be the worst and highest ranked demon out there, but he's terrible, and Levi lived with him for far too long. He worried he would become like him and at times, he is. A while back, right after Levi left our father's house, he wanted to make a name for himself. Being a demon was all he knew, so he became the worst one in town." She paused, clearly remembering those days. "Heidi and I tried hard to be a positive force in his life, and I think that we succeeded, but not completely. Here and there, I know he still uses his reputation to take advantage of people and situations, and sometimes he has to act on that reputation to show others he still has it." Her eyes misted. "If he was always this evil, then he hid it well from me."

"We never fully know a person."

"I would like to think I do know him. I would like to think something is causing him to lose his mind and act out of character."

I swallowed the last sip of my coffee. "The bond and I are the only variables in his life right now. That I know of."

Lacey frowned. "Maybe it is the bond. Maybe your feelings are disrupting his, and he is losing his mind and acting out of character."

That was a plausible answer, but I thought she knew that it ran deeper than that. A person couldn't be evil one day and good the next. It had to come from somewhere, from something.

Maybe the bond and the broken dam of unwanted feelings were the trigger, but that meant he always had evil inside of him.

"Either way, I'm stuck in here, while he's going in to get my wings by himself."

"A few of his demons are coming to help him."

I could help him. Hm, maybe I had an idea. I crunched the white bag and the empty coffee cup and pushed them to the side. "Lacey, could you break the circle?"

She stared at me with huge eyes. "I ..." Her jaw opened and closed several times.

"That tells me you can. So, hear me out. I think I can help him. He doesn't need to go in for a fight, but I need to get out of here to make that happen."

"I can't ... he told me not to. He threatened me."

"Has he threatened you before?" I asked. She nodded. "Has he followed through with his threats?" She shook her head. "Then I don't think he'll do anything to you. You're his little sister. He'll never hurt you."

"But what about you?"

I wasn't so sure about me. "Who's more important to you? Your brother or me?"

"Well ..."

I offered her a small smile. "Your brother, I know, and I wouldn't expect anything else. So, help me so I can help him. Please."

"I don't know ..."

I leaned back against the bed. "It's okay. I'm just offering. We don't need to do anything."

Lacey glanced at the door, as if looking after her brother. This was probably killing her and I felt bad for her, but only a little. I had no time for sympathy right now.

"If I break you out, how are you going to help him?" she asked, her unsure eyes back on me.

I had to fight a smile. I was going to win this one. "Do you have a phone?"

22

THINGS WERE GOING BETTER THAN I ANTICIPATED.

After my call, Lacey was about to break the circle, but before she could, Levi came back.

Levi fished regular metal handcuffs from his pockets and advanced on me.

"What's that for?" I asked, retreating.

"We're going to San Francisco."

I glanced at Lacey, surprised. Then it hit me. "Because of the bond."

He nodded. "Unfortunately, I can't go and leave you behind," he had said. If he drove up there and I stayed back, he would hurt.

Great.

He put the cuffs around my wrists, asked Lacey to break the circle, which she did, and lastly, he grabbed my upper arm and dragged me to the car like a criminal.

We rode mostly in silence, and I tried my best to keep my feelings neutral, my heartbeat slow, lest Levi realized what we were planning.

In two hours, we arrived at a townhouse in a residential area in San Francisco. A demon opened the door for us, clearly one of Levi's goons.

"How is it going, Burgin?" Levi asked.

"Everything is ready, sir," Burgin said.

We entered the mostly empty house, and Levi asked Lacey to draw a witch's circle in the middle of the living room for me. Thankfully, while she drew it, he let me use the restroom, and then handed me water and an apple.

"Thank you," I said, disdain dripping from my words and expression.

"It's for your own good, sweetheart," he whispered as he took off my cuffs.

"So, you found this empty house?" Very petty for a demon.

Levi glared at me. "If you need to know, sweetheart, it belongs to a friend. He has been out of the country for over a year now."

I was surprised he had answered me. I thought he would growl at me, maybe bark and snap his teeth.

Like a rabid demon.

Damn, clearly, I was still hating him.

Annoyed, Levi gestured to the circle. Knowing there was nothing I could do about it, I stepped inside, and Lacey completed the spell.

Damn, I was still trapped.

My agony grew with each passing second as Levi walked through the house, talking to his demons about his plan. I didn't hear much, as he didn't talk about it in front of me on purpose, but I got bits and pieces.

They would set up camp outside the mansion at

sundown, and near midnight, when they saw an opportunity, they would create a distraction and invade the house.

Levi had mentioned contacting a vampire hacker he knew. "He'll be able to take care of the security alarm for us."

Lacey also moved around a lot. She checked on me constantly, but she spent most of the time with Levi, though I had seen him shooing her away a couple of times, probably so she wouldn't know the plan's details.

Why? Was he afraid she would tell me? And what I could do from here?

While I was stuck in this circle, I could only worry.

Worry that this move, all of this time to think, had changed Lacey's mind and she wouldn't break this circle.

When sundown was near, Levi halted outside the circle. "I'll be back by morning with your wings."

I stared at him, my eyes full of anger, and didn't say one word.

He turned to Lacey. "You two should have dinner, and ... bring some pillows and blankets for Ariella. There should be some upstairs."

Lacey nodded. "Be careful."

He flashed a dazzling smile. "What's the fun in that?"

Then he was out, his demons following him. Two stayed, apparently to watch over us in case the angels or other supernaturals found me.

After we saw Levi's car leaving through the window, Lacey rushed to me. I didn't even have to ask. She worked her magic and broke the circle.

I sighed in relief as I stepped out of it. "Thanks."

"You're welcome."

"I have to say, for a moment there, I thought you had reconsidered our plan."

She nodded. "I had. But then I heard Levi's plan. He'll waltz in the mansion, search for your wings, and take them."

"That's not a plan. That's a wish list."

"Exactly, and from what I heard, the house is secured with modern technology and dozens of bodyguards. Levi is powerful, but even he has his limitations."

"Don't worry," I told her. "This will work."

She pressed her lips tightly. "Maybe I should come with you."

"What? No. If Levi sees you there, he'll lose it. He'll be reckless and do more stupid shit. No, you have to stay."

Lacey grabbed something from her pocket. "Take this." She deposited a small white pouch in my hand. "It's a bomb. Throw it near your enemies and it'll daze them for a minute. In case anything goes wrong."

A minute was enough for when I found my wings and had to run out of there. "Thanks."

"If I had more time, if I had known your plan, I would have done more for you."

"It's okay. Hopefully, I'll just need this." I fisted the pouch. I glanced at my phone, which had been recharged by Lacey on the car ride here. "It's almost time. I should go."

"Right. The demons Levi left behind are outside, one around the front, the other in the back. Be careful."

I nodded and approached a window in the back, on the house's left corner, where it met the wooden fence that separated the yard from the neighbor's. I opened it and spied out. The demon was across the long yard, looking out into the darkening horizon.

"Wait." Lacey crouched down and touched the tip of my boots. A rush of magic coursed through my feet. "You can jump and run now. No one will be able to hear your footsteps for the next ten minutes or so."

I smiled at her. "Thanks."

Not one for sappy goodbyes, I sat on the windowsill, climbed down, and jumped over the fence. I heard a little squeak as Lacey closed the window behind me, but I didn't stop moving. The next two houses didn't have a fence, so I could run straight through their backyards, until I was at a corner house, jumped another fence, and found myself at the street.

With my phone in hand, I used the map app to guide me out of this neighborhood to a busier street. It took fifteen minutes of fast walking, but when I got to the street, I saw a two-story medical building with two taxis parked in front.

I jumped in one, rattled the address to the mansion, and tried to relax on the thirty-minute drive.

Tricky thing to do.

Five minutes away, I called in. "I'm almost there."

"Good," was all the voice on the other side said.

My hands sweated and my heart thumped. The moment I got there, Levi would know it.

The taxi stopped right in front of the iron wrought gates. I paid the driver, stepped out, and faced the two demons behind the gates. "I'm Ariella."

The gates parted in the middle, rolling on side rails, and stopped with a six-foot gap. Swallowing hard, I walked past the gates. Immediately, they closed behind me.

I tried not letting that affect me as I continued down the stone path that led to the mansion.

Not even five seconds later, I heard his voice.

"Ariella!" I glanced back and saw Levi holding the gate

bars, his eyebrows at his hairline. "What the fuck are you doing?"

Four demons appeared from the side of the gates, pointing what looked like taser batons at Levi.

"Step away, demon!" one of the guards said, jerking the taser forward.

Levi bared his teeth at them. "I want to see you try."

The guard pushed the taser up to Levi—

"Wait!" I called out. The guard stopped, the taser just half an inch from Levi's hands. Damn it. This was not my plan. "He's with me."

Levi tilted his head.

The two demons who had been guiding me to the house stepped beside me. "Are you sure?" one asked.

I sighed, knowing I would regret this. "Yes, I'm sure."

The gate opened again. Levi growled at the guards before walking to me. He came to my side. "What the fu—?"

"Just ... stop it, okay," I whispered. "And behave, or I'll tell them you're *not* with me."

His eyes darkened and his jaw ticked. I knew this was hard for him, but thankfully, he dipped his chin once, and that was enough.

For now.

We continued following the two demons down the path. It curved around a beautiful garden and opened to reveal a huge three-story stone mansion.

In silence, the demons guided us to the big front doors, through a large, opulent foyer with a giant stone staircase, and a wide archway and into a sitting room with several green velvet couches adorned with golden details, heavy green curtains over the long windows, and a golden fireplace that was taller than Levi, where a fire burned, but didn't emit any heat.

"Duncan will be here shortly," one of the demons said.

Both of them walked out, probably to return to the gates, and left Levi and me alone in that giant seating room.

Levi was in my face, his eyes dark and cruel. "What the fuck do you think you're doing?"

"I'm saving your life," I barked back, trying not to raise my voice.

He scoffed. "Are you serious, sweetheart? Do you have that little confidence in me?"

"I think you were putting yourself unnecessarily at risk for something that doesn't even matter to you."

"You asked me to come with you. You practically ordered me, by summoning and creating a bond with me."

"I did, I know, and I don't regret it, but I hoped it would be easier to get in here. And thanks to the reward on my head, it was."

"What did you do?"

"What I asked you to do. I called Duncan, introduced myself, and said I would like to see my wings one last time before the angels found me."

"You did what?" his voice rose, along with his temper.

What I didn't tell him was that first Lacey had called one of his demons back in Houston to find out Lars's phone number. She then called Lars, told him she had the angel everyone was after, and she would only proceed if she spoke directly to Duncan. Reluctantly, he gave us his boss's number and I spoke to him.

Duncan was interested in getting a peek at me, the fallen angel who was causing a mess in the supernatural world, before I was captured and killed by my own kind.

"I have to ask two things," he had said. "One, aren't you afraid I might take you for the reward? And two, what was it that you did that has the angels running around like cockroaches?"

I thought for a second and decided that I should be as honest as I could. "I'm not afraid you'll hand me over for the reward, but that you'll keep me there along with my wings." I hoped he didn't know I didn't have my magic, otherwise he would certainly try. "As for what I did ... I saw something I shouldn't and they want to silence me."

That seemed to spark his interest, and he promptly gave me his address and told me to come this evening. When Lacey was about to break the circle in the cabin, I thought I would have to steal Levi's car and come to San Francisco by myself, even if it caused him pain.

Fate smiled my way, though, and Levi brought me here.

Now both of us stared at each other, ready for a fight.

"I knew I would be granted entrance that way," I said.

"Entrance, sweetheart, but no way to get out." He cursed under his breath. "This is a trap. He'll keep you here."

"Then, we fight our way out."

He narrowed his eyes at me. "That's exactly what I was trying to avoid."

"A fight? But you came ready to attack!"

"Without you! So you wouldn't get hurt!"

My heart squeezed; Levi was worried about me. That second ended and I remembered that if I got hurt, Levi could feel it, and that would make it harder to fight.

He didn't care about me or my wings or my magic. He only cared about himself. About getting the wings back so he could go back to his life.

"Right. I forgot you get hurt when I do."

"What?" His eyes rounded. "You think I'm worried about me?"

"Aren't you?"

He opened his mouth, but his gaze shifted to the archway.

A man with short blond hair and an impeccable indigo suit walked into the room. He looked at Levi for a few seconds, then turned his hazel eyes to me.

"Mr. Kensington, I'm Ariella. Nice to me—"

He raised his hand. "I know who you are and I don't believe we talked about you bringing a guest."

Rigid, Levi stepped closer to me, his hand on my back. "I couldn't let my girl walk into a stranger's house by herself."

His girl? Was he serious?

Duncan slipped his hands into the pockets of his pants. "Drop the act, Leviathan. I've heard about you and your reputation, and I know Ariella is not your girl. Though, I must say, I don't know why a higher demon is accompanying a fallen angel to my house."

"I asked him to come with me," I said, before Levi spewed out more nonsense. "We have business between us, and I was nervous about coming alone."

He narrowed his eyes at me. "I see. Well, should we find your wings?"

"I would love to," I said.

"Follow me, please." Duncan turned on his heels and moved into the foyer.

Levi glanced at me, as if I could read whatever he was trying to tell me. I shook my head and followed Duncan. He was on the first step of the wide stone stairs. Halfway to the tall ceiling, the stairs opened to a ledge and became two— one going to the right, the other going to left.

Duncan took the stairs to the left; Levi and I followed

him. The stairs led to a hallway that was as wide as my entire apartment back in Crosby. We walked by many archways to big art collection rooms and some closed doors.

With each step, my stomach turned and my chest tightened increasingly. I was within range of my wings, my precious wings that I had missed so damn much. I had to fight not to sprint past Duncan and find them myself.

A hand slipped into mine and gave it a little squeeze.

I glanced at Levi, but he was looking ahead, his attention on our host and his guards, who were certainly just around the corner. He had probably sensed my nervousness, my excitement, and he had held my hand.

I frowned. Damn, he was one confusing demon.

At the end of the hallway was the tallest, most ornate archway of all, but we couldn't see anything beyond it, just darkness.

Duncan paused a couple of steps from the archway. "Ready?"

"Yes," I said, my voice slightly trembling.

The lights came on, revealing a room with a large glass case right in the center, like an armoire.

Inside it were my wings.

And they were black.

23

―――――

I almost laughed in Duncan's face. "You're joking, right? These can't be mine. They are black!"

"Sure they are." Duncan walked into the room and stood beside the display. It was easily twice his size. "Once the wings are ripped, they turn black." A proud smile adorned his lips. "Do you know how rare it is to see black wings?"

Which meant, they cost a lot more than I first thought and his security around them was probably tighter too.

My stomach dropped. It might be difficult, it might cost my life, but I wasn't walking out of here without my wings, even if they were black.

I turned to Levi. "You knew they were black, and you didn't tell me."

"I thought you knew," was all he said.

Really? Did he think I was an angel with black wings? That was insane. I knew of only one angel with black wings and that was because he spent twenty years being tortured in the underworld.

Regardless, these were my wings. My eyes fixed on them,

and in a trance, I walked toward the display and reached toward it.

"No, no." Duncan pushed my hand away. "If you touch the glass, the alarm will sound and the doors will lock instantly."

I glanced back at the archway. "What doors?"

He pointed to the thin opening on the top of the archway. "An enchanted metal sheet drops from that fissure." He gestured to the ceiling where there were six round openings, the size of golf balls. "We can suck out all the air from this room or fill it with poisonous gas." He winked at me. "You wouldn't want that, would you?"

By the light, how was I getting my wings back?

My heart pounded against my ribs, the need to punch this glass greater by the second. I faced Duncan, desperate. "What is your price? Name it."

It would be millions, billions, and I had no idea how I would get that money. Did Levi have that much? Would he accept my soul if he got my wings back for me? Right now, I didn't care if he was a vicious higher demon. I would do anything!

"Some things are priceless, darling."

I whirled to the new voice and felt a punch to the gut.

Molraz.

"Oh, I forgot to mention I have a guest?" Duncan said. "Silly me. Ariella, I think you already met Molraz, the one who ripped your wings off."

"And destroyed her Celestial Sword, don't forget that," Molraz said, so casually, almost joking, as he walked under the archway and approached us.

Levi stood still as a statue, his eyes wide as he stared at

Molraz. Levi took a couple of steps back, until he was right by my side.

He grabbed my hand. "We need to go."

I pulled my hand from his and hissed, "Don't touch me!"

"Don't leave yet." Molraz halted a handful of feet away from us. He looked like I remembered, and yet, he was different. His black hair was longer now, to his shoulders. Back then, he had a short beard and now his face was shaved. But his intense blue eyes still shone the same. "The party is just starting. Now, you mentioned something about a price, darling."

The blood in my veins boiled. I couldn't believe I was facing Molraz again. I had dreamed of this moment so many times, envisioned it in my mind what I would do to him if I ever got a chance ... here he was and I was petrified in place.

"This will be fun," Duncan said, suddenly excited.

"The price for your wings is the Scarlet Hex Blade," Molraz said.

Of course it was. Why had I expected any less from him? From any demon for that matter?

"I don't have the dagger." It wasn't a lie. I hid it.

"That's a shame," Molraz said, his tone fake-dejected. Were all demons great actors? "Everyone here wants the dagger. I know Duncan would pay a great price for it." He stared at Levi. "How about you, son?"

It took me a moment to register what he said.

Everyone ... and son.

I stilled.

Levi turned to me, his blue eyes pleading. "Ariella ..."

"He's not just saying that, is he?" I must be going crazy. "Like when a person calls me child or dear. No, you're really his son."

"You didn't know?" Molraz laughed. "Oh my. Yes, he's my son and I believe you also met my daughter, Lacey."

So, he was the horrible father who had tortured his children. The one Levi had hated most of his life, and yet, ended up being just like him. Unless that was a lie too.

But it was true. I knew it; I could see it. The same black hair, the same straight nose, the same strong chin, the same tall and wide frame. Even the eyes were the same shade of shocking blue.

Wait ... how did he know I had met Lacey?

"Now the best part," Duncan muttered.

"I know something else," Molraz said, sounding awfully proud. "My son here is only helping you so you can lead him to the Scarlet Hex Blade. Isn't that right?"

The air whooshed out of my chest, and I took a large step back. I stared at Levi, my eyes round, my heart hurting. I had let him trick me from the beginning.

"Ariella, it isn't like that," Levi said, coming toward me.

I raised a finger. "Are you his son?"

He stopped and let his head drop. "Yes."

"Do you want the dagger?"

"Yes, but—"

I screamed. My heart raced, my blood boiled, my mind spun. I couldn't think, I couldn't act. I was in a room full of enemies, and the worst one was the demon I had let get close.

I rounded the glass display and went to the other side of the room, where I had a little more space for myself. I needed space, I needed time, I needed to think.

Levi had tricked me. He played me from the beginning. It probably wasn't in his plan to be bonded to me, but it had turned out in his favor, because with the bond, I would never suspect a thing ... why he was coming with me, why he was willing to help me. But the first time I went to him

...

"You knew who I was when I met you at that club," I said, my voice low. Levi stared at me. "But I didn't agree to your terms. I left. What would you have done if I hadn't summoned you?" He remained quiet. "Answer me!"

"I knew you were desperate and would come back."

"And if I didn't?" Again, he hesitated. "Don't lie to me!"

"I would have created an opportunity." He stared at me, his eyes pained. "I would have bumped into you outside Sylvie's house."

I pressed a hand to my chest. "You went to Sylvie looking for me."

Levi nodded. "Yes."

"Was she in on it?" She had been the one to tell me about him.

"No, she wasn't."

That didn't make any of this better.

Holy shit, it was all there. All the clues. I even remembered now how he mentioned a magical weapon, as if giving me an opportunity to confess about the dagger. The way he looked at me when that angel mentioned the dagger.

My knees weakened and I crouched down, breathing hard.

From the beginning, he knew who I was and all he wanted was the damn dagger.

Molraz had brought the Scarlet Hex Blade to Archangel Rhodes. We all had seen it, but we didn't know what the dagger was for, what it could do. Except Archangel Soren. He must have known because he paled when Rhodes held the dagger, and he called him traitor and attacked him.

Soren was able to take the dagger from Rhodes and throw

it to me right before Rhodes killed him. "Run," was the last thing he said.

Rhodes charged at me but Jeremiah and Rachel stepped in his way. Jeremiah and Rachel told me to run while they fought Rhodes. Shocked, I started running. It had felt like a betrayal to leave them behind, but if Soren had died to get this dagger out of Rhodes's hands, then I couldn't let him have it.

No one could have it.

I ran, but I heard Rachel's screams when Rhodes killed Jeremiah, and then she went silent.

I didn't get far, though. Molraz caught up with me. In our battle, he destroyed my sword and ripped my wings. Hurt and bleeding but still holding the dagger, I blinded him momentarily with my light magic and ran again.

I ran until I faced a cliff. I turned and saw Molraz, Rhodes, and all of the demons coming for me. I didn't think. I stashed the dagger inside my pants and jumped.

I thought I would die, but better to die from the fall, from drowning, than being caught by them.

Thankfully, I survived the fall and was able to get away.

I hid the dagger so no one would be able to get it.

Somehow, Levi learned I had the dagger before I even met him.

This hurt too much.

But I couldn't let it get to me. What was I going to do? Let them win? I hadn't given up the first time without a fight, and I wouldn't give up now either.

To hell with all of them. I might not have my wings and my powers, but I was a damn good angel, a strong one, and I was going to take them all down.

Even if I died trying.

Taking a deep breath, I stood and faced Duncan. "You never intended to keep me here; you sold me to Molraz." Then I looked at the monster who had taken my wings from me. "And you? What are you going to do? Sell me to the angels?"

Molraz showed me a dazzling smile that reminded me of his son's. It twisted my stomach. "You're smart, darling." He stopped right beside the glass case and looked at my wings. "And a great warrior. I still remember our fight. For a Cherubin, you were strong. Shame you chose the wrong side."

"And who is on that side? Rhodes is the leader?" My stomach tensed. "Did he take over Elysium already? Is that his plan? Or is Adona in on this too? If so, then to what end?" I shouldn't have asked but I didn't know anything about what was happening up there.

"Aren't you a curious angel," Molraz said. "I would love to answer all of that, darling, but soon, it won't matter. The angels have been contacted, and they are on their way to take you. You'll be tortured, and once they squeeze the location of the dagger from you—and trust me, they will—you'll be killed. No trial or other bullshit. Or ... you could spare yourself the suffering and tell me where the dagger is. I'll hold you until my demons retrieve it. Once I have it, I'll give you a quick, painless death."

Levi growled. "Don't tell him anything."

"Stay out of this, son. You're making a fool of yourself." Molraz's smile widened. "Did he tell you why he wants the dagger? Oh, wait, you didn't even know he wanted it."

"Stop it," I hissed. It didn't matter why he wanted it. He wasn't getting it and that was all that mattered.

"But it's such a happy story. Even if you're way out of your league, son."

"How did you know?" Levi asked, his voice trembling with rage. "How did you find out I was looking for the dagger?"

"Do you think all of your demons are loyal, son?" Molraz chuckled. "What's that line humans love to use in movies ... I have spies everywhere. It's true, you know. At least for me."

Levi's eyes darkened, and he clenched his jaw and hands, turning his knuckles white.

What did I care if Levi was mad? I needed to figure out how to get my wings and flee. I wouldn't be able to kill Molraz, but there was no time for that. I wouldn't win a fight against him and the angels were coming. I had to go before they arrived.

Live to fight another day.

Duncan leaned against the archway's pillar. "Such a good show. I should order caviar and champagne."

What a sick bastard.

"Your time is up, darling." Molraz's grin turned vicious. "Where's the dagger?"

"I'll tell you if you tell me what it does," I said.

Because there had to be something special about that dagger, otherwise why were demons after me to get to it?

Molraz chuckled. "Good one, darling. Nice try."

I glanced at Levi. "Do you know?"

Levi shook his head. "I know it's powerful."

I frowned. He had tricked me for a dagger. Why?

Shadows crackled around Molraz's hands. "Where's the dagger, darling?"

I shrugged. "Just kill me now, because I'll never tell you. I'll never tell anyone."

"So be it."

He threw his hand forward.

I took a step back and bumped into Levi, who wrapped

one arm around my shoulder and the other was outstretched, forming a shadow shield in front of us.

Molraz's darkfire exploded against the shield, sending tiny bolts of shadow everywhere. The bolts hit the glass case, breaking it into a million pieces.

The alarm echoed through the room and the metal door rolled down.

Molraz rushed out of the room, but Duncan pressed his hands against his ears and lost precious seconds.

The door closed, locking us inside this room.

Duncan took a sword from a display in the corner and pointed at us. "Stay back!"

Levi let his shield fade and lunged at Duncan like a bull. He easily sidestepped the sword's swipe, knocked it out of Duncan's grip, then wrapped his hand around the demon's neck.

"This is on you," he said with a snarl.

Shadows curled around Levi's hand and the demon's throat. He gasped for air for a few seconds, until his eyes closed and his head lolled forward.

Levi dropped him and his body fell to the ground with a heavy thud.

Then he turned to me.

I glanced around me, searching for a weapon. Then I remembered the pouch Lacey had given me. I slowly slid my hand inside my jacket's pocket.

He lifted both his hands, palms to me. "I won't hurt you."

"Says a demon who tricked me and just killed someone," I almost shouted, trying to be heard over the blaring alarm.

Levi shook his head once. "Look, we don't have much time. I bet my father is going to the security room right now to check the cameras and maybe even use the gas Duncan mentioned."

Shit, he was right.

I wanted to strangle him, but I had to be alive to do that. "I declare a truce until we're out of here."

"I'll take it." He turned to the wall and started patting it. "Now help me find a way out of here."

I wanted to, but the moment I looked at the broken glass case, I fell into a trance.

It was my wings. My damn, black wings. I hated that they had turned that color, but I had to admit, they looked so beautiful. Around me, the room disappeared, the alarm faded ... there were only my wings and me.

I walked to them and brushed my fingers against the soft feathers.

A current jolted through me and the next thing I knew, light magic swirled around my wings like twinkling stars, lifting them from their pedestal. On instinct, I turned and took off my shirt.

The wings wrapped around me and I sighed in relief.

Then they stabbed through my back and I screamed in pain. I fell to my knees as the pain spread and the wings attached to me once more.

"Ariella!" Levi skidded to me and knelt right in front of me. He reached for me. "What can I do?"

"Don't touch me," I rasped. I never again wanted him to touch me, and he was ruining this moment for me.

Yes, it hurt almost as much as when I lost them, but this moment ... I had lived for it for the last five years. It was all I wanted, all I dreamed about. I would endure this pain another one hundred times if it meant my wings were back and no one could take them from me again.

The pain lessened, but I knew it wouldn't go anywhere for a while, not until I got used to them again.

With a deep breath, I stood and spread my wings—they stretched ten feet wide. It barely fit inside this room.

Oh, my beautiful wings!

Tears blurred my vision and I wrapped them around myself once more, like a long-waited hug.

Levi's lips curled up in a small smile, the first one of this kind I had seen from him. "Beautiful."

I glared at him. "I didn't ask for your opinion." I folded my wings behind me and picked up my shirt. With effort—I hadn't done this in a while—I retracted my wings, until only two big, bloody gashes covered my shoulder blades. These too would heal with time, and the slashes would look like scars. I put on my shirt and turned away from Levi. "Getting out of here, remember?"

"Right," he mumbled.

I searched the walls, like Levi had done, looking for a switch or a hidden passage, while the alarm continued blaring.

"My father must be at the security room by now," Levi said. "The sick bastard must be watching us."

I stopped. "The security room ... like a control room." An idea came to mind. "Like a control." I knelt beside Duncan's body and checked his pockets. I fished a small rectangular remote control from inside his suit jacket. "Bingo."

I pressed a button and the alarm stopped. Jeez, that was so much better. Then I pressed another and the door rolled up.

"Well done, sweetheart," Levi said as he approached the door.

"Don't call me that." I put the remote in my pocket, in case we needed it again, and stood beside him.

As I suspected, a dozen demons stood right behind the door, probably sent by Molraz in case we were able to escape.

Knowing I couldn't fight them all, I threw the pouch Lacey had given me and it landed at their feet. White powder spread fast and the demons seemed drunk, wobbling on their feet.

I looked at Levi and gestured to the demons. "They are all yours."

He showed me his trademark grin and launched himself at the demons. For a full minute, Levi had his fun with the demons, taking out half of them before the time was up.

When the powder's effect was gone, one of them came at me. All right, I could handle one.

If I had my magic, though, I would kick all of their asses myself.

The demon rushed me. Remembering my training, I moved fluidly, spinning out of his swipes with grace. He lunged at me again, and I sidestepped him, entering one of the gallery rooms flanking the hallway. A bronze sword lay on a pedestal, just inside the opening.

I grabbed it, and when the demon came at me again, I swept it far, nearly tearing off one of his claws. He let out a roar that made the hairs on my neck rise. He went berserk. With his clunky movements, I ducked under his arm and pierced the sword deep into his chest.

The demon stilled, his eyes wide in surprise, and then he went down, sword and all.

Of course, by the time I was done with one, Levi had killed the others. And he had his phone to his ear. "Break in," he ordered. "Break into the house and attack anyone who crosses your path." He turned off and looked at me. "That should help us."

If his demons took care of the guards, we might have a chance of leaving this place alive.

As we ran toward the stairs, I remembered. "If you have traitors, your father might know they are coming in."

"I know, but it's all we have." He paused at the edge of the stairs. "Ariella, I—"

I shook my head. "Don't say anything. Let's get out of here."

His eyes stayed on mine briefly, then he nodded. We ran down the stairs, slowing at the landing when we saw Molraz in the middle of the foyer, on the way toward the front doors.

"Leaving already?" Molraz asked. "But the party just started."

Levi positioned himself in front of me as we climbed down the rest of the stairs. "Get out of the way."

"Or what?" His father chuckled. "Do you think you can hurt me, son? Kill me? I'm much stronger than you are."

Levi nodded. "That's what I wanted you to believe."

Molraz's smile faltered. "What are you talking about?"

"I hid the extent of my magic from you all of my life," he said. Molraz frowned. "I didn't want you getting any ideas of me joining you, becoming one of your lackeys, or worse, your associate. I didn't want anything to do with you then, and I don't want anything to do with you now."

"I'm impressed," Molraz said, sounding genuine. "A master's trick. I see the apple doesn't fall far from the tree."

"Unfortunately, it doesn't." Shadows covered Levi's arms. "Now let us go before I kill you."

Molraz tsked. "See, despite your pretty speech, I still think you're lying. And there's only way to know the truth."

Shadows surged up from the ground and flew at Levi like angry bees.

Levi grabbed my hand, jumping out of the way and taking me with him. We stumbled on the last step, and I let go of his hand, landing on my knees on the right side of the stairs, while Levi was five feet to the left.

Molraz didn't waste time. He created a shadow wall between us and wrapped a shadow snake around my arms and feet, picking me up from the floor and floating me toward him.

I struggled against his magic but couldn't move.

"Such a beautiful angel." I floated to his side and he reached up, twirled a finger around a lock of my hair. "It's a shame to kill you."

"Go back to hell," I said with a bark.

"And feisty. Darling, I like it." It sickened me how much Levi was like him. He grabbed a handful of my hair and pulled it back. "I promise, I'll make this painless."

"Let her go!" A roar shook the windows and the chandelier. Levi, in his full demon form, broke through the shadow wall and growled at his father. "Hurt her and I'll make you wish you were dead."

Molraz twisted me around, pressing my back to his chest and put a transformed claw around my throat and the other on my stomach. "Like this." He pressed his claws against my skin, and I swallowed a scream as his nails broke the skin.

A jet of darkfire bolts flew toward our feet, exploding into smoke upon contact, and making Molraz step back. In doing so, he loosened his grip on me.

I elbowed him hard in the stomach and then his chin. Groaning in surprise, he let me go and I fell hard on my hands and knees.

With a roar, Molraz cast a bolt of darkfire and pulled his arm back, ready to throw it at me.

I stilled, knowing this was it, and faced him. I wouldn't cower from death.

Levi rammed into his father, pushed him against the wall, and plunged his claws into his father's chest. "Good riddance," he said with his demon voice.

Then he pulled his father's heart out.

I GASPED IN SHOCK.

Levi stepped back, the bleeding heart in his hands, and watched as Molraz's body slid to the floor.

Slowly, he transformed back into his human form, his clothes gone, except for his ripped pants. He shook his hand, as if now aware of what he was holding and let the heart fall to the floor.

He stared at his father for one more second, then spun to me.

I didn't know what came over me. Bleeding, hurt, dazed, I jumped to my feet and ran. But before I could make it to the door, a dozen demons spilled into the foyer, all fighting each other. I dodged a pair, was almost hit by another, but finally made it out.

A handful of other demons fought, but now I had more room to run. Finally, the gates came into view and there wasn't a demon in sight.

"Ariella, wait." His voice was soft, almost pleading, so unlike him, that it took me by surprise. I halted but didn't turn to him. I heard his footsteps as he approached me. "About what happened—"

I spun so fast, I almost tripped on my feet. "Don't," I snarled. "Don't say anything. Don't try to explain it. I don't want to hear it. If it weren't for the bond, I would tell you to let me go."

His eyes locked on mine, the agony in them visible. Or was that another one of his tricks? He was still playing me. "If you're mad at me, then go. The pain will be punishment enough."

I could do that. It would feel like sweet revenge. But I was a freaking angel, and I should do better. "I can break it."

"The bond?"

I nodded. "Yes. I know how to undo it. But I'll need your sister."

LEVI TOLD ME TO GO TO THE CAR WHILE HE HELPED HIS DEMONS fight the mansion's guards. He explained he wanted to make sure they were all out of there before Rhodes and the other angels arrived.

Honestly, I thought about getting into the car and driving back to the townhouse. He could run back, for all I cared. But then I would get to the house and have to wait for him there.

I sank into the passenger seat, the adrenaline of the night wearing off, and the pain changing from a faint throbbing to a full burn. The pain was nothing, though, compared to the one good thing out of all of this: I had my wings back! I felt an urge to get out of the car and let them out again, so I could touch them, see them, feel them. To make sure it wasn't a dream.

But I could feel them inside of me right now, a faint sliver of magic, and that was enough.

For now.

When I thought I was finally relaxing, Levi came back, wearing a shirt he must have stolen from a dead body, and hopped into the driver's seat. He didn't say anything, and neither did I. Halfway to the townhouse, stopped at a red light, he started searching the center console and even reached over me into the glove compartment.

"What are you looking for?" I asked, annoyed.

"Pain medicine."

I glanced at him, but he didn't seem hurt. Oh, it was for me. He was feeling my pain and it was bothering him again. "Just wait a little longer, then you won't feel anything anymore," I snapped.

He fixed his hard eyes on mine for three seconds, until the light turned green, and he drove again.

The rest of the drive was silent, and when we arrived at the townhouse, Lacey rushed out to the front porch.

"Thank goodness, both of you are okay," she said, her expression relieved.

"You disobeyed me," Levi said, a bite in his words.

"It isn't the first time." Then, she lowered her voice and said, "It won't be the last."

If I had been feeling better, I would have smiled at her.

"I heard that!" he barked.

"Did you get your wings back?" Lacey asked me as I walked up to her. I nodded. "Then it worked out, didn't it? No need to be mad at me." Then she saw all the blood on me. "Oh, shit. Come in. I'll heal you."

I was in a rush to break the bond and leave, but I wouldn't say no to that.

Lacey guided me to the living room and patted a lone chair. I sat down and she hovered around me, her hands an inch from my skin, her magic tingling. She started with my neck, then moved on to my shoulder blades. I took off the blood-stained shirt, threw it in a corner of the room, and grabbed a clean one—and I cut two slashes on the back, so my wings wouldn't rip it when I called on them.

"I'm glad you got your wings back," she said. "That's good." I nodded but didn't say anything. Lacey glanced in the direction of the kitchen, where Levi had disappeared to, but we couldn't see him right now. "What happened that got his pants in a twist?"

I sighed. "Can we just get this over with?"

"Uh-oh, it wasn't good, was it? What did he do?"

Levi walked back to the living room and stood by the entrance, stoic like a statue. "Stop being so nosy."

She stiffened. "You're the one who brought me over. Again. If I'm curious about what's happening around me, it's your fault!"

I sighed. "Well, I found out the demon who destroyed my sword and took my wings is your father and—"

"What?" Lacey croaked.

"—apparently Levi knew. He was lying to me from the first time I met him. He was using me." I stared at him and I hoped he could see the hatred I felt. "Too bad I found out and now he won't get what he wanted."

"My father ..." Lacey inhaled sharply. "He was the one. Oh, no." She sounded really shocked and sad about. "And you, Levi. What the hell did you do?" Lacey asked, her tone sad.

Realizing Lacey was done with my healing, I put on my

shirt and stood. I didn't want to dwell on all of that anymore. "Lacey, I need your help to break the bond."

"Hm." She glanced at Levi, then back at me. "If that's what you want."

Hell, yes, it was.

I showed her the texts Hazel had sent me and we got to work. I had already gotten the necessary supplies so it was a quick set up.

Since we already had a broken containment circle drawn on the floor, Lacey fixed it. When everything was ready, Levi stepped into the circle.

"Now what?" he asked.

"Just stand there," Lacey said. "It should be quick." He nodded, his eyes on her. He was ignoring me. Fine by me. Lacey handed me a small pocketknife. "Here, you start."

I flipped the pocketknife open and pricked my finger with the blade's tip. I let a few drops fall on the circle's line and recited the Latin words for the spell, "*Ego liber vos. Vinculum confractus.*"

The line shone a faint white and Levi groaned. His jaw was tight and he pressed a hand to his chest.

"What's happening?" I asked.

"Don't stop," he said through gritted teeth.

"*Ego liber vos. Vinculum confractus,*" I repeated.

Levi fell to his knees, breathing hard.

"It's the spell," Lacey said, worried. "Bonds are powerful. It must hurt to break one." She waved at me. "You have to keep chanting."

"*Ego liber vos. Vinculum confractus,*" I said repeatedly. With each sentence, Levi seemed to be in more pain.

At some point, he partially shifted, his skin darkening, his hands tuning into claws.

Then finally, the white line shone bright. "Now!" Lacey yelled.

I crouched down, reached inside the circle, and placed my hand over his heart. "*Ego liber vos. Vinculum confractus,*" I said one last time.

A force like an implosion came from the circle and I fell forward, inside the circle.

"Oh no." Lacey grabbed my shoulders and pulled me back. I fell over her on the floor.

The light died out and the room went eerily quiet.

Levi was kneeling on the floor, his human hands fallen at his sides, and his chin on his chest. For a moment, I panicked he had died.

"Levi?" Lacey asked. She crawled to the side of the circle, which didn't seem broken, even though I had crossed over. "Oh, shit, Levi!"

He inhaled deeply, lifting his head, his eyes wide. "I'm fine. I'm fine." He coughed and rubbed his chest again.

I frowned. "Isn't it gone?"

He stared into my eyes, as if looking for the line that connected him to me. "It is," he said. "I can't feel you anymore."

I let out a long, relieved sigh.

"Then why are you rubbing your chest?" Lacey asked.

"Because this ritual fucking hurt." He pushed to his feet and glared at me from above. "Are you done here?"

Ouch. I stood, trying to hold on to my dignity. "I am." I turned to Lacey. "Thank you ... for everything."

"Wait," Lacey said. She broke the circle so Levi was free and turned to me. She picked up my hand and deposited three golden coins on them. "If you ever need anything, call me."

I closed my hand around them and nodded to satisfy her. I intended to lose those coins as soon as I left. I didn't want anything to do with Levi and his family ever again.

I grabbed my bag from the corner, hiked it up my shoulder, and walked out the door. I was proud of myself for not looking back once, even though I wanted to. I stopped at the end of the driveway, glanced right, then left. It was past midnight and the street was deserted.

What was I supposed to do now? Where should I go? How was I going to get my magic back? I was tired, hungry, and lonely.

Once more, I was all alone.

Right now, all I needed was to find a bed. After a good rest and some breakfast, I could worry about all of that.

My wings sprang to life behind me. I almost winced at seeing them black—it would take me some time to get used to it. Regardless, they were beautiful, they were mine, and I had them back.

With a big flap, I took to the night sky.

25

A Few Minutes Later

Ylena

I landed on the front steps of the mansion and folded my white wings behind my back. The two Seraphim who had insisted on accompanying me landed two steps behind me, their Celestial Swords out.

But all that greeted us were the bodies of three demons lined up beside the steps and their blood spread around the front yard.

Splendid.

I walked into the mansion and Rhodes stepped into the foyer. "Ylena, you're here."

I glanced around. More demon bodies were lined up in the dining room to my right, there was blood, turned furniture, and broken decorations everywhere.

"What happened?"

Rhodes lowered his head. Technically, we both were archangels, two of the oldest in Elysium, but he knew I could obliterate him with a snap of my fingers.

"Ariella and Leviathan killed Molraz and fled," he told me.

That was interesting. "Leviathan killed his father?"

"To save Ariella."

"Is that so?"

He nodded. "I've watched the security footage and that's what it seems."

I always thought Leviathan was like his father, but apparently the little demon had a heart, albeit a rotten one.

"On this footage, did she tell Molraz about the Scarlet Hex Blade?" Molraz always tried to get his own way. I was sure that if he could get the dagger back, he would hold it against me again. He must have tried extracting the location from her.

"No."

Damn it. My entire plan, the one I had been concocting for decades, could only be carried out if I got the dagger. Five years ago, I thought I had finally taken a turn and was on the last phase of my plan, when I sent a team of angels down to Earth for a double goal mission, none that they knew about: to retrieve the dagger from Molraz, who had actually asked for too high of a price, and to eliminate any higher-ranked angel who would never turn against Adona.

Then Ariella unexpectedly joined the mission.

And unexpectedly, she survived it, stole the dagger, stayed off our radar, eliminating any chance I had of finishing my plan.

It pained me to lie about Ariella, to make Elysium believe

she was a traitor, and to hunt her. She had been a pupil of mine, a bright student, with a fabulous career in front of her. I had planned on working on her, turning her to my cause.

But that time had been stolen from me, and now I couldn't afford having her tell anyone the truth.

"I think Ariella doesn't know you're involved," Rhodes said.

That was new. "Why do you think that?"

"I've watched the entire footage from the time she and Leviathan arrived to the moment they left and I heard her talking about me, asking Molraz what my plan was, why I wanted the dagger, if *I* had done something to Adona. But she never mentioned you."

Of course. Ariella saw Rhodes killing our people with Molraz's help, then she was cut off from our world. She didn't know anything that had transpired since.

I could use that to our advantage.

"Good, let's keep it that way."

"I know that face," Rhodes said. "What are you going to do?"

A delicious smile spread over my lips. "I'm going to have a little fun."

Enjoying Ariella's and Levi's story? Then don't miss book 2, Light Magic: https://julianahaygertbooks.com/products/light-magic

If you would like to read a short scene from this book from Levi's POV, you can download it here: https://dl.bookfunnel.com/ctlhhg1tnm

Haven't read about Hazel and Sean? Then check them out

here: https://julianahaygertbooks.com/products/the-midnight-test

How about Erin and Rey? I've gotcha you: https://juliana haygertbooks.com/products/the-demon-kiss

Also, join my Facebook group (https://www.facebook. com/groups/JulianasClub) to get another exclusive book, *The Light Witch*. The main characters in this book, Evelyn and Ash, will show up on book 2 of Shane+Raika's series!

Last but not least, you can check out the recommended here: https://www.julianahaygert.com/wp-content/uploads/ 2024/02/Rite-World-Reading-Order.pdf You can download, print, and check the books you've already read! Enjoy!

Academy book 1): a fast-paced story about a young woman who finds out she's a demon hunter, and the half-demon intent on protecting her against all evil.

The Vampire Heir (Rite World 1: Rite of the Vampire): a dark and mysterious paranormal romance about a vampire and a young woman with a secret.

The Warlock Lord (Rite World 4: Rite of the Warlock): a thrilling and kick-ass paranormal romance about a werewolf and warlock.

The Wolf Forsaken (Rite World 7: Rite of the Wolf): a heat-wrenching tale about a lost wolf shifter and a fae princess on the run.

Winter King (The Wyth Courts book 1): a fae king needs to sacrifice a pure-hearted human to save his kingdom from a terrible curse. Only, he soon finds out she's his fated mate.

Heart Seeker (The Fire Heart Chronicles book 1): an urban fantasy series about a young woman who finds herself at the center of a mysterious supernatural world.

Destiny Gift (The Everlast Series book 1): a post-apocalyptic urban fantasy series about a young woman with a special power that can save the world.

IF YOU WANT TO SEE EXCLUSIVE TEASERS, HELP ME DECIDE ON covers, read excerpts, talk about books, etc, join my reader group on Facebook: Juliana's Club!

ABOUT THE AUTHOR

While USA Today Bestselling Author Juliana Haygert dreams of being Wonder Woman, Buffy, or a blood elf shadow priest, she settles for the less exciting—but equally gratifying—life as a wife, a mother, and an author. She resides in North Carolina and spends her days writing about kick-ass heroines and the heroes who drive them crazy.

Subscribe to her mailing list to receive emails of announcement, events, and other fun stuff related to her writing and her books: www.bit.ly/JuHNL

For more information:
www.julianahaygert.com

facebook.com/julianahaygert
x.com/julianahaygert
instagram.com/juliana.haygert
goodreads.com/juliana_haygert
pinterest.com/julianahaygert
bookbub.com/authors/juliana-haygert
youtube.com/julianahaygert
tiktok.com/@julianahaygert

ALSO BY JULIANA HAYGERT

To find links and more info, go to:
www.julianahaygertbooks.com

Standalones
Daughter of Darkness

Rite World: Fallen Angel
Dark Wings (Book 1)
Light Magic (Book 2)
Fallen Demon (Book 3)
Wicked Angel (Book 4)

Rite World: Night Wolves
The Night Calling (Book 1)
The Night Burning (Book 2)
The Night Hunting (Book 3)
The Night Rising (Book 4)

Rite World: Vampire Wars
The Darkest Vampire (Book 1)
The Darkest Witch (Book 2)
The Darkest Magic (Book 3)

Rite World: Lightgrove Witches
The Midnight Test (Book 1)
The Midnight Spell (Book 2)
The Midnight Flame (Book 3)
The Midnight Secret (Book 4)
The Midnight Hunt (Book 5)
The Midnight Wish (Book 6)

Rite World: Blackthorn Hunters Academy

The Demon Kiss (Book 1)
The Hunter Secret (Book 2)
The Soul Bond (Book 3)
The Shadow Trials (Book 4)
The Infernal Curse (Book 5)

Rite World
The Vampire Heir (Book 1)
The Witch Queen (Book 2)
The Immortal Vow (Book 3)
The Warlock Lord (Book 4)
The Wolf Consort (Book 5)
The Crystal Rose (Book 6)
The Wolf Forsaken (Book 7)
The Fae Bound (Book 8)
The Blood Pact (Book 9)

The Wyth Courts
Winter King (Book 1)
Spring Warrior (Book 2)
Summer Prince (Book 3)
Autumn Rebel (Book 4)

The Fire Heart Chronicles
Heart Seeker (Book 1)
Flame Caster (Book 2)
Earth Shaker (Book 2.5)
Sorrow Bringer (Book 3)
Soul Wanderer (Book 4)
Fate Summoner (Book 5)
War Maiden (Book 6)

The Everlast Series
Destiny Gift (Book 1)
Soul Oath (Book 2)
Cup of Life (Book 3)
Everlasting Circle (Book 4)

<u>*Willow Harbor Series*</u>
Hunter's Revenge (Book 3)
Siren's Song (Book 5)

<u>*Breaking Series*</u>
Breaking Free (Book 1)
Breaking Away (Book 2)
Breaking Through (Book 3)
Breaking Down (Book 4)